D0385694

All
PETS
ALLOWED

ALSO BY ADELE GRIFFIN

THE OODLETHUNKS:
Oona Finds an Egg
Steg-O-Normous
Welcome to Camp Woggle

WITCH TWINS:
Witch Twins
Witch Twins at Camp Bliss
Witch Twins and Melody Malady
Witch Twins and the Ghost of Glenn Bly

VAMPIRE ISLAND:
Vampire Island
The Knaveheart's Curse
V Is For . . . Vampire

All PETS ALLOWED

Blackberry Farm 2

Adele Griffin
pictures by LeUyen Pham

Algonquin Young Readers 2021

Published by
Algonquin Young Readers
an imprint of Algonquin Books of Chapel Hill
Post Office Box 2225
Chapel Hill, North Carolina 27515-2225

a division of
Workman Publishing
225 Varick Street
New York, New York 10014

LIBRARY OF CONGRESS CATALOGING-IN-PUBLICATION DATA

Names: Griffin, Adele, author. | Pham, LeUyen, illustrator.
Title: All pets allowed : Blackberry Farm 2 /
Adele Griffin ; pictures by LeUyen Pham.
Description: First edition. | Chapel Hill, North Carolina :
Algonquin Young Readers, 2021. |
Audience: Ages 7–11 | Audience: Grades 2–3 |
Summary: "When Becket and her twin brother, Nicholas, adopt new
pets from the local shelter, Becket's dream dog turns out to be a
super-shy scaredy-pooch, and Nicholas's cat is more outgoing and
attention-seeking than he was expecting"—Provided by publisher.
Identifiers: LCCN 2021010641 | ISBN 9781643750736 (hardcover) |
ISBN 9781643752297 (ebook)
Subjects: CYAC: Brothers and sisters—Fiction. | Twins—Fiction. |
Pets—Fiction. | Country life—Fiction.
Classification: LCC PZ7.G881325 Al 2021 | DDC [Fic]—dc23
LC record available at https://lccn.loc.gov/2021010641

10 9 8 7 6 5 4 3 2 1
First Edition

For Archer

CHAPTER 1

Countdown!

WANT TO HEAR SOMETHING EXTRA-LUCKY? MY TWIN brother, Nicholas, and I are turning ten on October tenth!

Ten on Ten Ten!

That's some unbeatable, unrepeatable birthday luck, and we've just got to make the most of it. I've had city birthdays all my life, so moving out to the countryside and Blackberry

Farm this year has changed everything. Country living means roosters and fields instead of pigeons and subways, and a whole new way to run, shout, and play birthday games.

Nicholas doesn't use up his energy the same way as me, but he said yes to all my farm-tastic game suggestions: Capture the Flag; Mother, May I; Red Light, Green Light; What's the Time, Mr. Fox; Blind Man's Bluff—and his fave, Musical Chairs.

We are also serving our fave lunch: grilled cheese sandwiches with crusts cut off (me) and plain yellow-mustard sandwiches with crusts on (Nicholas). Dessert is a combo of Nicholas's and my top choices—one layer of yellow cake (me) plus one layer of chocolate cake (Nicholas) with lemon filling (me) and chocolate fudge frosting (Nicholas) plus sprinkles (me) and vanilla ice cream (me) and mango sorbet (Nicholas).

Guests leave with goody bags of my favorite treats (yo-yo, ink stamp, face eraser, and tattoo sticker), along with Nicholas's favorite treats (candy

jewel ring, tiny cello charm,
and saltwater taffy).

"Three more days
till our Top Ten Ten
Takeover!" I shout from
my bedroom. I started our birthday countdown
when it was forty days away. I can't believe we only
have three more days to go.

"Three more days till too
many kids, loud noises, and
sparkler candles!" Nicholas
calls back.

I don't know if Nicholas
means that to sound happy or
anxious. Probably a bit of both.
When it comes to big birthday bashes—ours
or anyone else's—Nicholas can get "hanxious."

For example, Nicholas did enjoy our Nine Lives
birthday party last year—right up until the cake.
As soon as we lit the sparkler candles, Nicholas
yelled, "Put out the sizzle fire before the house
burns down!"

3

Then Mom and Dad blew out the sparkler candles, and we had a do-over with regular candles.

Nicholas mostly had a good time at our Eight Your Brains party when we turned eight. We had a zombie theme, but then my friend Caleb showed up wrapped head to toe in toilet paper. He looked so much like a real zombie that Nicholas hid in the bathroom.

Nicholas is also nervous about this year's party, but he wants the Top Ten Ten Takeover to work out. We are both new at Boggs Hollow Elementary, and having the best birthday party of the year is a sure way to show that the Branch family is here for fun! (Especially Becket Branch, who planned this whole exciting party!)

Or so I think, until Nicholas makes his big announcement.

"Could I have a small family birthday party as my main party?" he asks casually as he takes one of Dad's homemade blueberry muffins from the basket. "Sort of like the one we had when Becket and I turned seven?"

"What!" I almost choke on my sip of orange juice.

Nicholas turns to me. "It was fun, remember? Pizza and bowling? Then, Becket, you can host the big class party Saturday."

"I love this idea," says Mom. "Two parties. One family party, and the Saturday social one."

"I'll make pizza," says Dad.

"Nooooo wayyyy!" I'm shaking my head. "The magic of this birthday is how the day matches the month AND our ages! It has NEVER been more important for us to show up as twins!"

"Don't listen to Becket," says our big sister, Caroline. "Do what you want, Nicholas."

Nicholas has found his old fidget spinner, and he is playing with it under the table with one hand. Only I can see. I've told him he's got to keep that fidget spinner at home—it's so kiddish, especially since we're at a new school—but he just hides it in his pocket instead. "What do you want, sweets?" Mom asks Nicholas.

Nicholas is quiet. My eyes are begging him.

"Oh, Becket." Caroline sighs. "Why is it that every year you have to make your birthday party the most important thing in the universe?"

"You had everything you wanted on *your* birthday," I remind her. "You got a necklace and a fancy bakery cake and your best friend celebrating everything about you!"

"My party was a fraction of the size of yours," says Caroline.

"Nobody asked me to be a twin," I say. "But since I am one, I have an obligation to double the fun. Nicholas and I aren't just turning ten years old—we are turning twenty years old!"

6

That doesn't sound right. "You know what I mean."

"Follow your heart, Nicholas," says Mom.

"Follow my heart a little bit, too," I add.

Nicholas's voice is very small. "Okay," he says. "As long as it's not too noisy, and you keep Travis away from me, and I don't have to play any ball sports, I guess I'll be fine." He looks at Mom. "So I take it back. We don't need a family party. I'm cohosting with Becket. Top Ten Ten Takeover! Just like how we planned."

"Thanks, Nicholas!" When I fling out my arms to hug him, I knock his fidget spinner out of his hand. Nicholas catches it just in time. "This will be the best party ever, promise!"

Nicholas nods and clears his throat. "Best party ever," he echoes, but his owl-wide eyes look like he's imagining all the ways it will go wrong.

CHAPTER 2

Easy Out

DAD MADE THE MUFFINS, SO MOM DRIVES US TO SCHOOL, and Dad will bike to the Old Post Road Animal Clinic, where they both work. They are splitters like that. Nicholas sits up front, and Caroline and I are in the back. Nicholas gets carsick, so we are quiet while he closes his eyes and listens to his Mello-Cello playlist all the way to school, which, unfortunately, sounds like the funeral part of a movie.

I've saved my chewable vitamin to eat in the car. One day, scientists will discover that chewable vitamins are just gummy bears for breakfast, but till then, it's a Beautiful Alert in my morning mouth. The first time I ever shouted "Beautiful Alert!" was back in kindergarten, when I blew all the seeds off a puffy white dandelion. For me, it was a way of noticing and being thankful for something extra-good. Even if I don't say my Beautiful Alerts out loud so much anymore, I'm still keeping watch.

I clean the fog off my glasses, open my sketchbook, and read:

BRANCH TWINS TOP TEN TEN
TAKEOVER PARTY TO-DO LIST

1. Invite Whole Class ✓
2. Excellent Outdoor Games ✓
3. Yummy-for-Tummy Birthday Foods ✓
4. Fun Toys in Goody Bags ✓

I uncap my marker and add:

5. Don't Stop My Bop Playlist TO PLAY NONSTOP

Twenty favorite songs pop and jingle into my brain in no time—my pen can hardly keep up.

Nicholas is squeezing his nose, because marker smell makes him dizzy. He turns in his seat to face me.

"What's all that squeaking about?" he asks in a stuffy-nose voice.

"My pen is making a playlist," I say. "Want to add any songs?"

"Beethoven and Vivaldi," says Nicholas. "Everyone loves relaxing tunes mixed in with the loud stuff."

"Cool." I write down:

6. Olden-Day Music to Play at the End, When
    Everyone Is Going Home

Our invites went out weeks ago, so that grown-ups could have the phone numbers and directions to Blackberry Farm, but last night Nicholas and I made each kid in the class a paper ticket that reads ADMIT ONE FOR BIG BRANCH FUN!

I personalized every ticket, and they are suitable as keepsakes.

Nicholas was in charge of drawing his specialty—a seven-color rainbow—and licking the envelopes.

Before lunch, our teacher, Mr. Dragan, lets me walk around the desk pods and deliver my ticket envelopes to the whole class: Frieda, Kefele, Royal, Cadie, Zane, Jay, Archer, Lennon, Penelope, Siddy, Ash, Linus, Travis, and Skye.

I drew an alpaca on Frieda's ticket, because her family has an alpaca farm. I sketched floofy bunnies on bunny-loving Kefele's ticket, and a narwhal for Travis, because he has a narwhal lunchbox, and I painted cookie circles on Archer's ticket, because Archer would eat homemade chocolate chip cookies for every meal.

Who knows if I'm the best artist in the fourth grade? But I am definitely the artist who makes the most art. While I'm passing out the tickets, kids start saying "Ooh!" and "Thanks, Becket!" I make sure to call out, "Nicholas did the rainbows!" I'm feeling as happy as a dog with two tails until Travis says, in a pretend-curious voice, "Hey, Becket, why did you draw me a flying frog that's got water spouting out of his head?" Then I wish I could uninvite him to the party, or at least take back his ticket.

Later, we have gym outside, and Coach Valentine lets us vote for kickball. I love kickball. I get to third base on my kick, but when Nicholas is up, the outfielders walk in close.

"Easy out, easy out," they chant. Nicholas

kicks two fouls before he wobble-kicks the ball—
nooooo!—to first base. I sprint home safe, but
Coach Val calls, "Oooout!" and Nicholas slumps
for the bench with his face crunched into a frown
like he's trying not to cry.

I'm pretty sure I hear Travis say, "Hurts to
be yoooou!" Travis does that to everyone, but
it's still embarrassing when he says it right to
your face.

On the bench, Nicholas's best friend, Zane, and
I sit on either side of my brother. His head hangs
low, and he is scuffing the toe of his sneaker on the
ground.

"You get big points for trying,
Nicholas," I tell him.
"Being at gym class
is way braver than
skipping gym to
read comic books
in the nurse's
office, like you
did last year."

My twin looks up at me hot-eyed. Like it's me, not Travis, who did something wrong. "I can't believe we're gonna have all these outdoor games at our party," he says, his voice shaking a little, "and I'm no good at playing any of them! Kids will laugh at me, watching me mess up for my whole birthday!"

"I thought you were okay to play some outdoor games."

Zane cuts in. "Hey, Nico. What if we do something else fun. Did you know 'Deep Pit' is playing over at Hawthorn Cinemas? Let's go to the matinee! My treat. We'll get Frootyslurps. I want to find out if Captain Brink gets out of that slime pit."

"I can't skip my own birthday party," says Nicholas. "We're having mustard sandwiches and mango sorbet and Vivaldi."

"But you told me you never have fun at any of your birthday parties," says Zane. "You said Becket plans noisy bad ones, and then makes you go."

"Wait, what?" I shout. "I'm not making Nicholas do anything! Right, Nicholas?"

14

Nicholas just gives me those wide, anxious owl eyes. He's got his fidget spinner out. My heart sinks.

Zane frowns at me. "He told me you want him to make a wish for the gift that *you* want."

"Nicholas, *our* birthday wish was a secret!"

"I didn't say it exactly like that," mumbles Nicholas.

"'Deep Pit' will be better than Becket's loud, yelly party," continues Zane. "They used almost a million pounds of pit slime."

Out of the corner of my eye, I see Travis sneaking over. I jump up from the bench. "Travis, nice try! I can see your SuperSquid."

He is not supposed to bring his squirting toy squid to school, but Travis never lets rules get in the way of his pranks.

"Identifying heat," says Travis in a robot tone.

"Identifying smell," I say, but Travis ignores me.

"Travis, what do you need?" asks Zane in a warning voice, but Travis isn't scared of anyone, not even big kids like Zane. Besides, Zane is more of a quiet giant who is a lot like Nicholas on the inside.

"I need nothing. But. Mr. Crybaby. Needs. A. Squidly. Cooldown." Still pretending to be a robot, Travis raises his SuperSquid a couple of inches and sprays Nicholas with a shot of water right in the face.

"Nooooo!" sputters Nicholas. Travis snickers and darts away before Coach Val or Mrs. Salami, the teacher's aide, sees.

"That kid is such a jerk," says Nicholas, wiping his face with his shirt. "Thanks for trying, Becket."

"See, this is why Nico doesn't want a birthday party," says Zane. "Because you invited Travis to it."

"Because I had to invite him! It's a whole-class invite!"

But Nicholas looks sweaty and sad. Squid water is dripping off his chin. Suddenly I get a brain flash of how a big party might feel through Nicholas's eyes. The music. The kicky games. Travis's pranks. It's pretty awful to hear that Nicholas has been saying one thing to me and telling Zane something else.

"Follow your heart, Nicholas," I say in a loud voice so Zane doesn't miss a word. "It's your birthday, too. I want you to spend it however you want."

CHAPTER 3

Sizzle Fizzle

MY ALARM CLOCK BEEPS ME AWAKE, AND I'M OUT OF BED IN a flash to check on the weather. Birthday Beautiful Alert! The sky feels extra-wide and birthday blue, with a couple of fluffy clouds wandering across like stray sheep. Perfect party weather.

Still in my PJs, I head to the barn to feed Pickle and Chew, our donkey and mule. Pickle and Chew love their breakfast so much they don't even mind when I get them in their sandwich-board birthday signs.

Pickle gets a HAPPY BIRTHDAY, BECKET sign, and

18

Chew is wearing HAPPY BIRTHDAY, NICHOLAS. Aw, they look so cute!

"Thanks for the birthday wishes!" I tell them.

I collect ninety eggs from the henhouse— nine times ten, a magic birthday number!—and I take them to the mudroom that is connected to Branch's Farm Store. We clean the eggs and pack them into cartons here to sell along with the dairy and bakery items made by our neighbor farmers. I'm gently placing the last egg in the rack for Gran to wash when it slips through my hands and lands, *crack-splat*, on the flagstone floor.

Eighty-nine eggs? That's not an even birthday number. Is a broken egg bad birthday luck? I clean up the egg as best as I can, but it's hard to get all the sticky off the surface. I know that Gran—who lives above the store, which is exactly five stone's throws from our farmhouse—will help me out by giving the floor a better, grown-up cleanup later. That's just the kind of Gran she is.

It's still early when I get back to the house to check off my chores on the chore board. Dad is in the kitchen. He's just popped the cake pans in the oven, and now he's starting to make the frosting. "Happy birthday, Becket!" he says.

"Thanks, Dad!"

"Happy birthday, Becket!" Gran is here, too, holding a bunch of morning glories from the garden. She finds a vase in the cupboard and sets the arrangement on the table.

"Thanks, Gran," I say, but my heart tugs. Mom has a kitchen wall calendar called *The Meaning of Flowers*. June's flower was morning glories, which according to the calendar mean "love in vain." Did Gran just bring some sad-flower luck into the house? Luckily, when I sniff, all I smell is baking cakes and melting chocolate. "I wish I could eat cake for breakfast," I add.

"Speaking of breakfast," says Gran, "I think Chew likes his birthday sign a little too much." She points out the window.

Oh no! In the pasture, Chew's sign is sticking out of his mouth.

I dash outside. "No chewing, Chew!" By the time I pull it away, the sign just says HAPPY BIRTHDAY, NICH.

More bad luck? I hope not.

"Happy birthday, and I'm sorry, Nich," I say when I return to the kitchen. Nicholas has come downstairs dressed in his I PLAY THE CELLO—WHAT'S YOUR SUPERPOWER? T-shirt and his shorts with the silver rockets. I hold up his sign scrap. "I tried."

"Happy birthday, and it's okay, Becket," he says. "I won't be here, anyway." Zane's parents are taking the boys out for a birthday breakfast before the matinee. I'm disappointed that Nicholas decided to skip most of the party, but everyone else is cheerful about it, so I'm trying to be okay with it, too.

"As long as you're back in time for cake," says Dad. He has moved on to make the cake filling, and the frosting is cooling in a bowl. The whole kitchen smells like a fancy bakery. I don't know how Nicholas can bear to leave!

"I'd never miss the cake," says Nicholas. "Or the wishing," he adds. "I'm ready to blow out those sparklers. The distance between ten and nine feels longer than the distance between nine and eight."

I give him a thumbs-up. But is it more bad birthday luck that my one and only twin won't be here for our party? Especially when Nicholas and I discussed combining our wishes for the one thing we both want most?

A few minutes later, when Zane's family drives up, Nicholas rushes out the door. He doesn't even look back when I call, "Goodbye, have fun!"

"Whoa. He really didn't want to be part of today's racket," says Caroline.

"Not racket," I say. "Celebration!"

"Whatever," says Caroline.

It's not until I'm dressed in my rainbows-and-penguins shirt plus my new cargo pants with six pockets (you can never have too many pockets) and I see the first car pull up our driveway (yay, it's the Francas!) that I'm back in the spirit.

"You brought Oro!" Oro is Frieda Franca's golden retriever. He's a dog superstar who knows all the tricks:

roll over, fetch, play dead. Plus he can catch a Frisbee in his mouth, no matter where you fling it.

"Happy birthday, Becket," says Frieda's big sister, Daisy.

"Race ya to my room before the fourth-grade brigade shows up." Caroline grabs Daisy's hand. "I've got two new sets of press-on nails with decals." She sweeps Daisy off, but not before Daisy presses her finger to the freckle at the end of my nose. "Where's your wonder twin?"

"He went to the movies with Zane," I say.

Daisy looks confused.

Caroline says, "This is way more Becket's party."

I'm about to protest when Dad points me to the door. "Host, we need you up front, please. More guests are coming."

I take a deep breath. The way I always saw it, Nicholas would be on one side of the door, me on the other, and each of us would throw a handful of homemade ripped-up paper confetti on every guest who walked in. I used wood pulp paper, which is the best paper for the environment, and it took me almost two hours to rip.

But, hey—I can still make it work!

I scoop up a handful of confetti and throw it on my head for good luck, and then I grab more handfuls to toss on all my guests.

Woo-hoo!

For the next couple of hours, my party is fierce birthday fun. Even Gran gets into it. She comes outside to be the referee for Capture the Flag. Every time it feels like we are winding down, someone else thinks up another fun game.

No bad luck here, after all.

"Everybody! Watch this!" Ash throws a piece of popcorn in the air and catches it on the tip of his tongue like it's a snowflake.

"It's snowing, it's snowing!" calls Cadie.

"A blizzard in October!" Linus tosses a handful of popcorn in my face.

"Look out," I shout. "I'm the Abominable Popcorn Monster!" We make a huge popcorn snowstorm. Then we jump in leaf piles and pitch armfuls of leaves at one another, until I am so tired that I lie down on my back, staring up at miles of birthday-blue sky. My tiredness covers me like a blanket of rainbows.

In the distance, I hear a honking horn. I jump to my feet.

A blue truck is winding up the driveway.

Penelope wails, "Ooh nooooo! It's my mom!" She hops out of her leaf pile and beelines for the house. I follow. "She's coming to get me early, for my gymnastics class—and now I'll miss the cake! Unless we can have it right now."

"I can't do it if Nicholas isn't here," I say.

"Cake! Cake!" chant Royal, Jay, and Lennon as they follow me into the kitchen. Everyone cheers as Nicholas and Zane—right on time!—step inside through the back door.

"To the porch!" commands Gran.

"I'll take the pictures," says Caroline, who always takes the pictures.

Kids smack on their party cone hats and squeeze around the table. I slide onto my half of our chair, and Nicholas sits in the other half—just like every year.

Everyone starts singing the happy birthday song. The twenty-two sparklers (ten apiece plus

one for each of us to grow on) are crackling and popping. But Nicholas is trembling at my side. Under the table, I take his hand.

"These sparklers are smaller than last year," I whisper. "Hang in there."

Here is our big twin secret: We are wishing for a DOG. We want a dog more than anything else. Okay, I might want this dog a little bit more than Nicholas.

28

But it's such a big wish, we decided to share our wish power.

I squeeze Nicholas's hand a little harder. We decided on the wish last month. My heart pounds with the word: *dog, dog, dog, dog, dog, dog, dog, dog, dog, dog*, ten times, and one big *DOG* to grow on. Nicholas's hand is sweaty. I don't let it out of my grip.

At the end of the song, everyone chants: "Are ya one? Are ya two? Are ya three?" All the way up to "Are ya TEN?"

"TEN!" I yell. I take a humongous breath.

"Make a wish!" my friends call. The sparklers hiss and pop.

Dog, dog, dog, dog—Nicholas jumps up to a stand and hops back from the table like it's on fire.

Oh no! Am I supposed to do all this sparkler work alone? I blow so hard it hurts. *Dog, dog, dog, dog*—one candle sputters back to life.

"Identifying heat!" calls Travis.

29

SSSSSSSS. The sparkler goes out in a puff of wet smoke.

Kids start to boo. Oh no—this is birthday bad luck for sure!

"Nooooo!" I yell. "Why, Travis, why?"

Travis steps back, holding his SuperSquid. "Everyone knows you can't keep even a single birthday candle lit," he says. "Then ya don't get your wish! You're welcome, birthday twins!"

CHAPTER 4

A Helping Hen

OUR CAKE LOOKS LIKE IT GOT CAUGHT IN THE RAIN. IT SMELLS like burnt matches. My friends leave most of it untouched in damp lumps on their plates. Mom's face is all frown, and I have a feeling from the way she is tapping her phone that she is texting Travis's parents. But Travis is not a kid who cares about getting in trouble.

"If I hadn't helped you with my SuperSquid, you wouldn't be getting your

31

wish," he says loudly, after his mom and dad make him apologize.

"Enough, Travis," his parents say at the same time. They don't let him take a goody bag, either.

"I doubt it matters how the candles went out," says Nicholas hopefully.

He's probably right. But my spirits feel as soggy as half a leftover cake.

"Did you do the wish ten times?" I ask.

Nicholas frowns and clasps his hands behind his back, like he's trying to remember. "Oh. Uh-huh."

When everyone is gone and we're done with the last of the cleanup, I keep hoping Mom or Dad will say, "Actually, kids, there's one last thing we wanted to give you!" I jump into different rooms, searching for any sign a dog might be trotting into the house. A rawhide bone, maybe? A freshly filled water bowl?

Dad comes up from the basement

with a basket of laundry. "Who wants to lend me a hand?" he asks.

"Aha!" I yell, and I dive to it, to check for anything warm and fluffy hiding.

But the only thing warm and fluffy in the basket is laundry.

"Since you're feeling so energetic, why don't you help me fold, okay, Becket?" Dad winks. "Many Branches, one tree, right?"

Ugh. Folding is officially one of Nicholas's chores, but the other family rule is you always help out when you're asked. I reach in for a T-shirt.

Later, I go down to the henhouse to feed the hens.

"Godiva, you might just be my only pet for a while," I tell her.

Gran says Laying Godiva likes me best because I am in charge of her breakfast feed, and because I keep the henhouse so clean and swept.

Sometimes, Godiva even sits on my lap, but right now she is on her regular perch, her head tilted, listening.

This past summer, after our pug,  Mr. Fancypants, died of the olds, Nicholas and I were sad for a long time. I'm still sad, in a quieter way, and I sleep with Mr. Fancypants's collar on my desk, so I can see it every night before I fall asleep. But it's hard to live on a farm and not imagine how happy a new pet would be here.

Nicholas always says he would be glad for a dog *or* a cat.

All I want is a dog.

I used to think I wanted a big, smart, floppy, happy, loyal, energetic dog—like Oro Franca. I'd made a vivid picture of that dog in my imagination.

I'd even named him Noble O'Keeffe Branch, after my favorite painter.

But the more time I've spent without a dog, the more I realize that any dog is an excellent dog. Really, it is the quality of a dog's dogness that is most important. A hen isn't a dog, but a hen is feathers and friendship—and that counts, too. I bet I could teach Godiva to fetch. Maybe I'll bring a tennis ball to the henhouse tomorrow. Or a Ping-Pong ball! Godiva could roll it around with her beak. She could even learn how to roll it to me.

How much can that old hen do?

Especially with a good teacher like me. We'd figure it out!

Godiva feels so warm and soft that she puts me in the exact right comfort space. Together, we watch the sun setting, as orange as cheddar cheese, through the slats of the henhouse.

CHAPTER 5

Hint of a Gift

THE NEXT MORNING, THE WHOLE FAMILY—MINUS GRAN, WHO is checking inventory at the store—is outside in the orchard. Raking and stuffing leaves into compost bags is one of many Branch family outdoor chores. Mom and Dad say that Branches love outdoor chores like peanut butter loves jelly.

Still, Nicholas has been taking plenty of sit-down breaks and water-bottle breaks, and Caroline is kind of overdressed for the day, in her denim skirt and leaf tights, and she has orange pumpkin and yellow maple-leaf decals glued onto her fake nails.

Caroline's trick is to look like she's part of an activity when she mostly wants to take artistic pictures of it. She has to rake really slow so her nails don't fall off, and she keeps picking up her phone to get a close-up dramatic photo of a twig or of Nicholas staring thoughtfully into the distance, not working.

But I love group activities, so I was made for chores! Plus composting is a way to recycle leaves by adding their nutrients back into the soil.

What a Beautiful Alert thing to do for the Earth!

I work quick, and I finish two bags for each one Nicholas and Caroline fill.

"Great job, kids," says Mom, after we've hauled everything around back to compost. She checks her watch.

"Oh, look at that. It's time."

"Time for what?" I ask.

"Time to pick up your birthday gift o' clock," says Dad.

"AHHHHHHHHHHHHHH!"

I start yelling so loud it's like there's no end of the sound inside me. I run in zigzags between the crabapple trees. Even after I loop back, my whole yell is not out.

"All right, Becket," says Dad. "Save some of that energy for the trip."

"You don't even know what your twins gift is," says Mom.

I stop in my tracks. Did I just hear "twins gift"?

Birthday gifts are a ton of fun. But Mom and Dad have been known to get twins gifts wrong. I've been dropping hints like crazy, but my parents have their own ideas of the perfect twins gift. Two years ago, it was a photo album of Nicholas's and my baby pictures, bathtub bums and all. Last year, it was matching plaid pajamas. We looked like a pair of mini lumberjacks.

Nicholas's face is hopeful. Come to think of it, our baby photo album is in his room. Also, he loves those lumberjack PJs.

"Give us a hint," I say.

"I have some guesses already," says Nicholas. "Is it a sled?"

"Nope," says Mom.

"Is it a tree house?" he asks.

"Not this year," says Dad.

"Is it a telescope?" he asks.

"Ooh," says Mom. "But no."

"Is it an ice cream maker?" he asks.

"No," they say together.

"Wow, good guesses, Nicholas," I tell him. I had no idea my twin had such a big wish list inside him.

"We give up," I say, so that Nicholas can't keep guessing all day.

Mom and Dad trade one of those parent looks of pure enjoyment.

"You'll have to come with us to find out," says Mom.

Caroline is staying behind with Gran, who has closed Branch's Farm Store so they can make a nice lunch for Daisy and Mai. They are on the Pumpkin Patch planning committee for Boggs Hollow Elementary and

Middle Schools. The Pumpkin Patch is a fair that happens every fall at Boggs Hollow. Since Nicholas, Caroline, and I are new at Boggs Hollow, we've never been to a Pumpkin Patch, but already I'm looking forward to it even more than Halloween! It's all that the kids talk about—the rides and games and food tables—and the profits always go to help the school. This year, we are raising money for solar panels. Nothing stripes a rainbow across my heart like pumpkin patches, outdoor fairs, and helping my new school go green!

"By the way," I remind Caroline, "if you need to learn anything cool about solar energy for your play date, we're studying it in Social Sciences class—so I know a lot of fun facts."

"First—um, no thanks. Second—middle schoolers are way too old to have play dates," says Caroline. "The term for what I'm doing is 'hanging out with my friends.'"

"You're wearing your favorite tie-dye sweatshirt," observes Nicholas. "So even if it's not a play date, it's something."

"Yeah, it's tie-dye-sweatshirt-worthy," I say.

"Stop making this into a *thing*." Caroline looks embarrassed, but she still plumps the couch cushions and refolds the throw blankets.

We leave just after Mr. Franca drops off Daisy and Mai. Daisy is Caroline's friend from the summer, but Mai is Caroline's new friend from school, who was just voted class president. Lately, we have heard a lot about Mai around the dinner table.

"Gran is baking us brainstorm banana bread," Caroline tells the girls, who are coming in through the front as Nicholas and I head out the kitchen door.

"Save some for us!" calls Nicholas.

The car trip will lead us to our twins gift, and it doesn't take long for me to guess where we are going. When we pull off the highway at Exit 8, in the direction of the North End Animal League and Adoption Center, my hopes start rocketing. Even my fingers and toes feel overactive. I get out my doodle dog notebook and look at my list:

WHY I SHOULD HAVE A DOG

1. I already take care of the Blackberry Farm animals (Laying Godiva and all the chickens, plus Pickle and Chew) by feeding and grooming them, checking them from ears to tails, and making sure their water is fresh, with no dead bugs on top and no yuck stuff at the bottom.

2. I handle all moth, ant, fly, and spider body removal and toilet-flush burials for Nicholas.

3. When Mr. Fancypants was old and sick, I was in charge of him.

Next to me, I see that Nicholas has gotten out his kitten notebook. I peer over his shoulder, and to my enormous surprise, I read:

WHY I SHOULD HAVE A CAT

1. I am already in charge of the laundry and the laundry room, which is a good place to keep a litter box.
2. I like the smell of catnip.
3. I enjoy the indoors, soft objects, and cello music (same as cats).
4. I am good at clipping my nails, so it will not be hard to clip a cat's nails.

A cat? Say what now? We don't want a cat! Also, what a bad list! For one thing, how does Nicholas know what music cats like best? Also, why would a cat care if Nicholas also likes catnip? Nicholas's list is more about how cats remind Nicholas of himself. Not about why he should have one.

"Nicholas," I say. "Did you remember to wish ten times for a dog?"

"Sorry, no," he says uneasily. "At the last second, before I got too scared that the sparklers would burn down our house, I wished ten times for a cat."

"That wasn't the plan."

He shrugs. "Cats make me feel peaceful," he says. "They're independent souls. But they also pick favorites. Like, I'd want my room to feel like my cat's home base, too, even though they're nocturnal. That would be so cool, right?"

Nicholas's reasons for a cat are very Nicholas-y, but—it *has* to be a dog! I prefer dogs very loudly. Nicholas might have a kitten notebook and a JUST HANG IN THERE poster, and he might still wear the kitten-face bedroom slippers I gave him last Christmas—even though his feet got too big—but a dog is more of a family pet. Besides, Mr. Fancypants was a dog, and Nicholas LOVED him. A dog is for everyone.

We are here. My legs are shaking. I can't handle the suspense anymore!

"Dad! Mom! Which is it going to be?" My yell breaks loose. "What pet are you letting us get? Tell me now! I can't take it!"

Mom and Dad are both smiling. "We've always said that when the time is right, we would add a cat or a dog to the Branch household," says Mom. "But Dad and I have talked about it, and now think that we can handle a—"

"Cat, cat, cat!" squeals Nicholas.

"Dog, dog, dog!" I shout.

"Actually?" says Mom. "Both, both, both."

My yell comes roaring back! I've just got to run another loop, all around the outside of the North End Animal League. Joy is stinging in my eyes, or maybe it is the ferocious smell from the garbage dumpsters behind the building.

Just when I think one loop is enough, my sneakers decide to run the loop all over again.

"Becket," calls Dad. "Come back to us, please."

I stop. I'm panting.

"Mom and I also thought if we adopt the pets together, they'd have a better chance of adapting to each other," Dad is telling Nicholas when I rejoin them, panting like a dog, dog, dog!

"I really like this idea," says Nicholas in quiet wonderment. "I can't believe it. A cat. For me."

I feel light-headed. Five minutes ago, we were

a family with zero house pets. Soon we will be a family with two pets! It's too much!

I'm not prepared for this much happiness!

My skin is so warm. I can hear my heart beating in my ears.

"Let's go find our pets," says Nicholas solemnly.

"I need a minute!" I am still panting.

But then Nicholas takes my hand, and with him, I feel ready.

CHAPTER 6

First Dibs

"THANKS FOR VISITING NORTH END! COME MEET OUR FAMILY."
A curly-haired young person wearing a green shirt
with a name tag that says ANGEL looks from me to
Nicholas. "Are you cat people or dog people?"

Nicholas says, "Cat" at the same time I say,
"Dog."

Angel smiles. "Cats and dogs are opposite but
compatible. Let's go."

Mom and Dad's vet friend, Dr. Herschel, is
working in the front office today.

"Give yourselves some time," says Dad. "Mom and I will be in here."

The shelter is big and echoing.

"It smells nice," says Nicholas. "I'm glad there's no dog-poop smell."

I sniff. It's true. The shelter smells a little bit like kibble and a little bit like bleach. I can feel a lot of  animal liveliness, even though all I see are crates and just the shadows of movement from the dogs or cats inside. For some reason, I'd imagined that the animals would be roaming in packs, doing whatever they wanted. But the space in here is more like a giant-sized version of the back of the vet's office, where the x-rays and surgeries happen.

It's an animal orphanage, really. I am quiet, thinking about the importance of adopting. I'm giving myself one chance, and I'm also giving a dog one chance. Animals are not the same as shoes, where if you get the wrong size or color you can just exchange it. If you bring an alive animal with feelings into your home, you want to be sure you're both the right fit for each other. It's kind of a big deal.

I wish I spoke dog. My ears wriggle as I try to crack the bark code.

Aroo-roo-roo! Beck-urf, Beck-urf!

Pick me! Pick me! Please, please, please! I'm your dog!

So many dogs in this shelter are in need of love and care. How can I possibly decide on just one? I lap the rows of crates while keeping my eyes straight ahead. I wonder if there are other forces here, guiding me. I don't want to get myself too upset about all the animals I don't pick, but part of my heart is in a permanent tug because I can't adopt them all. What if all it takes is one millisecond of eye contact, and I bond with a dog instantly and forever? Then what?

Because once I bond, it's very hard for me to unbond. I've got to be careful.

Down the aisle, a kid in a faded red hoodie, plus his grown-up, are peering down at a crate. "Look—this one's called Star. He's got a white star mark on his forehead!" says the kid. "Hey, Star!" He straightens. "Maybe I like him best. But what if there's a better one somewhere? Actually, that marking on his face makes him look kind of crooked."

A better one? What's better than a friendly face and a lopsided star marking? I don't even like the word *better* when it comes to comparing dogs.

"Let's explore the whole shelter before we make any decisions," says the grown-up. "We want to connect with the perfect dog."

The *perfect* dog? All dogs are perfect!

Nicholas has slipped away to the cat aisle, but Angel sticks at my side.

"It's good that you've got an outside run," I say when we stop at the back of the building and stare out the big, scratchy glass window. A bunch of dogs are chasing after balls thrown by green-shirted volunteers.

"Keep watching them as long as you want," says Angel. "I'm going to check in with your sibling."

I squint. I close one eye, then the other. Then both. Can I hear my special one and only dog, barking just for me? I need to feel where to look. I stick my hands in front of me, using my outstretched fingers as a guide, as I do a loop around, listening.

On my second loop, I bump right into Angel and Nicholas.

"Becket, why are you walking around with your eyes closed?"

I pop my eyes open. "Because I am trying to find my pet by its bark language!"

"I guess I just found mine the regular way. They call her Tiger. It was love at first sight."

The enormous amber-eyed, striped cat in

Nicholas's arms really does look like a baby tiger. "She's huge!"

"Otherwise known as the perfect size," says Nicholas.

Awl-Roo-oo-O-OOO-oooooo!

I turn to stare through the metal bars of a crate, and into a pair of eyes that are the same glossy brown as Dad's homemade fudge frosting.

"Awl-ROO!"

Star's raggedy ears are pricked up. There's a lopsided white star mark on his forehead. It doesn't make his face look crooked, just mischievous! He bounces in place. *Will you be the one to take me home?* is how that bounce feels to me.

"Would the dog in there want to meet this cat out here?" I ask Angel.

"More importantly, do you want to meet that dog in there?" Angel asks me.

I think I do. I crouch down. "Hey, buddy. You've got a lot of spring in your step!" Seeing a living creature jammed up in a small space reminds me how it feels when I'm at my desk during Sustained Silent Focus class. It is so hard to keep my body still during SSF—also known as Something Smells Funny, because that's the class where Travis lets go of his worst lunch burps.

Star whimpers. *Thump, thump, thump,* beats his crooked tail like a bent asparagus.

I peer up at Angel. "Yes," I say. "I want to meet this dog."

As soon as Angel opens the barred metal door, Star bounds straight into my arms, and for a moment, I am merged—part Becket, part lovable ball of coppery fur, shaggy ears, crooked asparagus tail and soft, slobbering tongue. It's pretty easy for me to stand up while holding on to this dog. He is floppy but sturdy, and he weighs about as much as my backpack when it's full of homework.

Nicholas's cat stretches out a paw. Tiger bats Star's ears. Then Star pitches forward, and his wide-tongued kisses nearly cover the cat's pointy face.

"They're saying hi!" I can't get over their friendly if different dog-cat body language. "Do they know each other?"

Angel is typing into a tablet. "Funny thing—they probably don't. But Star and Tiger were brought into the shelter on the same day. Both of them were found on the side of the road, about a mile apart. The cat was probably domestic, but turned feral. She had a broken leg that needed a splint. The dog was fully domesticated. We doubt he'd have made it another week in the wild." All the smile lights go out of Angel's face. "We get a lot of that."

"A lot of what?" asks Nicholas.

"Abandoned animals. People who want a pet just for the summer. Then they let them go 'free.'" Angel makes air quotes. "Letting an animal loose means putting it in danger. House pets are easy prey for coyotes. So it's unusual this cat managed to live for some time on her smarts."

"Amazing," says Nicholas. "A warrior cat."

"As for Star," says Angel, "he shines when he feels safe. But he scares easy. He's young, so he can learn new rules. He's got a lot of love to give a family that loves him."

Nicholas and I inch nearer together, so that the cat and dog can sniff each other out. Just then the red hoodie kid comes wheeling around the corner.

"Hold up! Is that Star?" The kid's lower lip thrusts into a pout. "It *is* Star! That's the dog I wanted! That's *my* dog! Dad, tell them!"

"We did have our eye on the, uh, brownish-red dog. With the crooked white star marking," says the kid's dad.

In my arms, Star is panting nervously. Like he can sense the tension.

"Not too big. Not too scrawny," says the kid. "Not too quiet. Not too growly."

"But, unfortunately, too late," says Angel apologetically. "Our rules give first dibs to the person who asks to see the dog out of crate. I'm very sorry."

"Hey! I'd wanted to check out *all* the dogs first." The boy sounds pretty ticked off, with a dose of bratty.

"This dog picked me," I tell him. I challenge his stare. He looks away. When he looks back up, I've still got my glare-stare on him.

Star is in my Favorite Names sketchbook. It's a strong name choice for this adorable dog. But the North End Animal League and this kid have already named my dog Star.

How is my dog *really* mine unless I choose his name?

"I'm renaming Tiger," says Nicholas firmly. "She's the most important thing I've ever been given—so I'm calling her Given. It's a name that always will remind me to be grateful for her."

"Good one, Nicholas," I say, meaning it. But now the pressure is on me. My brain swirls with all the other names since I picked Noble, my favorite dog name for almost a year. Since then, I have added Bagel, Rocket, Shadow, Peeper, Pixel, Peanut, Tater, Java, Snicker, Noodle, Bean, Wink, Kit, Bolt, Spade, Dune . . . and Butterscotch.

For every dog, there is a best dog name. Big dog, skinny dog, watchdog, jumping dog, silly dog. None of those names equals the crooked star marking and kinked tail and bounce of this specific dog.

My dog feels like he knows I'm thinking about him. His body has gone quiet. It's almost like he's listening to my thoughts. He has stopped panting, too.

The boy slinks away from me, giving one last

backward wistful look at "his" dog all cuddled up in my arms.

Too bad. I had dibs on this dog, and this dog has dibs on me, too. I nuzzle my nose into my new pet's soft, warm neck.

"Hey, friend," I whisper. "I think I'll name you Dibs."

CHAPTER 7

This Home Is Your Home

UP FRONT, MOM AND DAD SIGN SOME PAPERS.

"Dibs and Given have different dispositions, but they've got interesting stuff in common," says Angel. "They're both about the same age—between three and five years old. They're both about twelve pounds. And since they both came into North End on the very same day, March 18—they've got the same birthday. Because that is the day we put them on record."

"They're TWINS," I shout. "I have never heard a luckier thing happening to anyone who walked into an animal adoption center, ever! Twins adopting twins!" I turn to Nicholas. "Can you even believe this luck?"

"They can still have different birthdays," says Nicholas.

"Sure," says Angel. "You're in charge of everything about them now."

"I DON'T THINK SO!" I say. "Why would I ever turn my back on such a Beautiful Alert as pets with the same birthdays?"

"Your pets survived hard times, living out on their own," says Angel. "Every day is a celebration for a pet that feels safe and cared for."

"Any other tips?" asks Nicholas.

"Given thrives on attention," Angel tells us. "And Dibs seems to like music. If you hum or sing to him, sometimes it calms him down." Then Angel tosses me a small pink tennis ball. "Dibs and I were working on a trick. See if you can get him to balance this ball on his nose."

"Thanks," I say, and I pocket the ball.

On the way home, Mom and Dad talk to us about how Nicholas and I are 100 percent in charge of the pets. "We've got the clinic, and Gran's got the store," says Mom. "So we're already a busy family. You need to pull your weight."

Nicholas's owl eyes are worry mirrors. "I've never been totally responsible for a pet on my own," he says.

"We've got this, Nicholas," I say.

"I just hope we learn how to understand them," says Nicholas.

"You're just overthinking it," I tell him. "We understand them already!"

WE MAKE A BIG racket coming into the kitchen!

Everyone is carrying something—pets in carriers, bags of kibble, cans of wet food, a scratching post, a toy mouse, a chew bone, and two comfy saucer beds that we picked up at

Schneckenburgers' Dry Goods in town—deep forest green for Dibs and plaid for Given.

"What pet did you get? Let's see! Show us!" Mai, Daisy, and Caroline are all jumping and clamoring for a peek.

"Meet Given!" Nicholas sets the cat carrier on the kitchen counter and pops it open. Given leaps out like the freed mini tiger she is.

"That's some cat!" exclaims Mai. "What a predator!"

"Actually, a warrior," says Nicholas.

Daisy reaches out to touch her, and Given bonks her head against Daisy's hand.

"She does that with me, too," says Nicholas. "She's superfriendly, especially for a half-wild cat."

BONK!

"Tiger stripes are my favorite," says Daisy.

"That cat is all muscle," says Mai.

"Maybe she really *is* part tiger," says

66

Caroline. She keeps her hands clasped together as she leans forward to see. "Do you think she's dangerous?"

"Oh, no!" Nicholas rushes to rescue Gran's vase before Given's powerful tail nearly topples it.

"So let me get this straight. You two compromised on one pet?" asks Caroline, her voice slightly disbelieving. "And you agreed to get a big cat—that's the size of a small dog?"

"Actually—presenting Dibs!" I say. "He slept in my lap part of the way, and he's still sleeping in his carrier. Come on out, Dibs!" I've put Dibs's carrier on the ground. I unzip the top. Then I unzip its other side.

"Three ways to exit," I say. "Out you go, Dibs. Time to meet everyone."

But Dibs won't budge.

Dibs still won't budge when I set down a bowl of water, using his new bright-yellow bowl, which I place in front of the carrier.

And Dibs won't budge even when I dangle his new chew bone in front of him.

"Okay, let's try this a different way," I tell him. "Let's go outside." I zip the carrier back up and take him outside so we can sit on the bottom step of the porch. "How do you like this sunset?"

Before we lived full-time on Blackberry Farm, we would visit Gran for holidays, and I could never pick my favorite season. I still can't! Spring, summer, fall, and winter—each is a different paint box of Beautiful Alerts. But if I could only make one single painting, I'd use the colors I see today. I'd mix my thick, happy acrylic paints to fire up my pink and red apples, yellow piles of leaves, and blue wide-open sky. While I'm staring at the sky, a V-shaped wedge of geese passes overhead. I close my eyes to take a picture for my memory scrapbook.

"Here, boy. Come enjoy the fresh air!" People think that dogs being color-blind means they just see in black and white, but my parents told me that dogs are actually limited-spectrum, which means they see a different range of colors. Imagine a fall day through a dog's eyes, with violet-blue grass and laser-green apples!

But Dibs won't budge. Not even for a sunset.

It's not how Dibs acted in the shelter. I guess it's a big adjustment, trading a crate and a kennel for a new home and a new life as Dibs Branch.

"The rules around here are easy, Dibs," I tell him. "They are . . ." But I have to think about it for a minute. "Move around! You're an inside-outside dog. Check out how much space we've got! No crates, no cement, and no more all-gravel doggy runs."

Dibs cocks his head at me, looking confused.

"So let's run! C'mon!" I jump up and start running across the field. "The air will feel so good on your face!" I dash and gallop all over the place.

When I turn, the dog carrier is just a shoebox on my horizon.

I whistle between my fingers, how Gran taught me this summer.

It took me three weeks to learn to whistle like that. It does the trick!

A little snout pokes from the carrier.

I whistle again. Dibs pops out! Barking and running, he's a turbocharged streak of copper straight into my arms, where he plants a big, slobbery doggy lick over my whole face. I can feel his heart pounding wildly.

"You did it!"

Dad has come out onto the porch. "He can get some speed when he wants!"

At the sound of Dad's voice, Dibs does a funny thing. He turns right around and bolts across the field, all the way back into the carrier. When I catch up to him, I hear him from inside, panting soft and fast, the way I'd imagine a bunny rabbit would breathe.

"It's okay, Dibs," I say. "No need to panic. That's just Dad." I sort of sing it, to make Dibs feel soothed.

I zip up the carrier and haul it on top of my shoulder.

"Becket, I think Dibs likes your voice better than mine," says Dad. "So for now, I'm going to try to be quiet around your dog, while he gets used to us, okay?"

"Yes," I say. "He won't be shy for long. Right, Dibsie?"

Inside the carrier, Dibs has gone very still.

CHAPTER 8

The Big Idea

RIGHT AWAY, DIBS LETS US KNOW THAT HE'S SHY ABOUT LOTS of things. He won't go up or down the stairs unless I carry him. When Daisy shakes some kibble into his bowl, he won't eat it. He slinks into his crate when Mai and Caroline laugh too hard, or if he hears a door slam, or if he hears dogs barking on TV.

He is definitely not sure about Dad's voice.

"There's things in Dibs's past that we'll never get to the bottom of," I say. "I wish he could talk."

"You don't need to know his past," says Gran. "You just need to show up for Dibs now."

"Given is in Dibs's bed," says Nicholas. "Are you okay with that?"

"As long as Dibs is okay with it." I peer in at Dibs, who is in his crate. He doesn't seem to care about where Given is. Aren't dogs territorial?

Maybe Dibs doesn't know what his territory is yet.

"Given is gorgeous. That cat should be on a calendar," says Mai. "Doesn't it seem like she's posing for a calendar picture right now?"

"It does," says Daisy. "I can see the hashtags!

Hashtag 'CalendarCat.' Hashtag 'TigerCat.' Hashtag 'MeowStyle'!"

"What's cuter than twelve months of Given?" asks Caroline. "Wouldn't you love to see her peeking out from under a Christmas tree? Or wearing a Fourth of July neckerchief? You could fluff her hair, or tie a ribbon around her neck and put her in a basket. Everyone loves when a pet is fresh and clean and looks like a present."

"That's it!" Mai snaps her fingers. "That's what we'll do for our Pumpkin Patch booth! A pet spa!"

"A pet spa?" Caroline squeaks. "As in, with live animals?" My sister really likes taking photos of animals. She loves her animal nail press-ons with decals, and she likes animals on journals or posters. She would be first in line to own a *Given Branch: Twelve Months of Cat-itude* calendar. But when it comes to the muck and mud and smelliness of real animals and the chores that come with them, Caroline keeps her distance. That's why her board chores are things like make the salad and sort the recycling.

"Yes! A pet spa!" says Mai. "Because everybody

loves animals! We can give them pet-icures and purr-ty them up! All pets allowed!"

"I can contribute our tin washtub—the one we use to wash Oro," says Daisy excitedly. "It's big enough for a Saint Bernard."

"Ooh, ooh, ooh!" Mai snaps her fingers. "I bet my uncle can give us a ton of towels. He owns Top Shape Gym in town."

Caroline doesn't say anything.

"I'll make posters!" I announce into the awkward silence.

"Thanks, Becket," says Daisy.

"I do all the animal chores here," I add. "So

if you need any help, call on me!"

Caroline's smile is like a peeling nail decal. Even though I'm not Caroline's twin, I can guess what my sister is thinking. A pet spa means dander, sharp claws—and pet breath! If she doesn't want to do a pet spa, she should speak up—or I will for her.

"Caroline can do the money," I say. "She's great with money. She works the register at our store."

"Yes!" Caroline jumps in. "Just put me right in back, behind the cash box."

"The cash box?" Daisy looks doubtful. "That's just a tiny side job."

"The money part is the easy work," says Mai.

"It's not, when there's a rush at Branch's Farm Store," I say. "You need to be good with numbers and keep a cool head. And there's always that person who pays in loose change."

Mai chews her bottom lip. "I mean, but you've got to deal with pets, too."

"Of course! Becket just meant, I can *also* do the money," says Caroline. "Nothing's more fun than styling the pets!"

"We've got Mane 'n' Tail shampoo to contribute," I add. "That's what we use on Pickle and Chew."

"Cool," says Mai.

"This is going to be so fun," says Nicholas.

The oven timer pings. Gran pulls multiple loaves of banana bread out of the oven.

"I made six total," says Gran. "Five for the store, and one to inspire." She shakes one of the loaves from the baking tin, and soon each of us has a warm, chunky slice. But the moment he hears the clatter of the small plates, Dibs jumps in my lap.

"Solar panels are clean, green energy," I sing. "Our school is going to look amazing. You should see the artist's rendering, Gran."

I love singing out that Beautiful Alert phrase: *artist's rendering.*

"Cheers to green energy!" Mai raises her bread, and then it's gone in three bites. "We should make a list of services and prices. Let's name our spa, too."

"Wag Zone," suggests Daisy.

"Fancy Tails," says Caroline.

"The Fluff and Puff," says Mai. She sits up straight in her chair. "Because the rhymes are fun, the words describe what happens at a spa, and it feels cuddly."

Mai gets all the votes.

"A landslide win for the Fluff and Puff!" calls Nicholas.

Mai smiles and does a shoulder shimmy that I know I'm going to try to copy later—in private, up in my room.

Meantime, Given is still jumping from chair to table to lap, snuffling for banana bread crumbs. Everyone can pick her up and pat her, but she won't stay with anybody for too long.

Even when Nicholas gives her some treats, she doesn't stick to him.

Dibs stays in my lap, and his body goes tense when Mai's parents arrive to pick her and Daisy up. I set him on the ground to see if I can get him to eat. He puts his nose in the bowl, but as soon as it slides across the floor, he skedaddles away. So I get one of Mom's woven place mats to set under it. Solved!

When Dibs slips outside for his night pee, I have to stay with him and hum a tune so he knows he's not alone. It's really dark, with only a sliver of moon to shine on the different textures of the night. He circles and sniffs, sniffs and circles, but right before he is about to pee, he has to stop what he's doing to check in on me. Then it's like he's forgotten why he's out there. He has to start sniffing and circling all over again. Waiting for him is a chore!

"Dad is setting up Dibs's crate in your room," says Mom, who is waiting for me when I come back inside. "But first, you are going to wash all my woven place mats. I can't believe you put my nice mat on the floor for the dog."

There's no arguing with Mom. I wipe down all the place mats, and then Dibs follows me up the stairs.

He sits on my fuzzy slippers and watches me brush my teeth.

As soon as I snap off my lamp, Dibs starts whining and panting from his crate. When I let him out, he puts his front paws up on the side of my mattress and then clumsily hoists his wiggly-waggly heavy-breathing body right up onto my bed.

I sit up, snap on my lamp, scoop him up, and put him back in his crate. "Dibs, you might injure yourself if you fall off the bed, okay? Got it?"

Dibs's eyes are sad. But he seems to get it.

I snap off the lamp.

A couple of minutes later—hello! Guess who's back on the bed? On goes the lamp. Off goes the dog. Off goes the lamp.

On jumps the dog, and then— w h o o p s i e ! — Dibs slips and falls off the bed. He is panting hard, but when I snap on the lamp and check him for bumps and ouches, he seems fine.

Should I lock him in his crate? I scooch him back in, but I leave the door open.

Less than a minute later—*rustle, rustle*—Dibs is up on the bed again, belly-crawling along my side, burrowing, and even nosing a couple of my stuffed penguins. I place my hand on the back of his head.

Dibs goes still.

Hand off, and he's back to belly-crawling.

Hand on. He stops.

Hand off. Crawls.

I close my eyes. His fur is soft beneath my fingers. But his breath is shallow. As soon as I shift my hand an inch, Dibs is inching his way up the side of the bed, bopping my penguins onto the rug, one by one.

I lean over the edge.

"Penguins, I'm sorry," I tell them. "Maybe you can think of my rug as an Antarctic ice floe."

Dibs shapes himself into a doughnut and immediately is snoozing away. But as soon I fall asleep, I start dreaming I'm getting attacked by a snail. I wake up and feel—eeeyuck—Dibs panting and licking my neck!

"Yuck!" I pull up the covers so that he can't get to me.

He's not having a good sleep. Neither am I. It's not until I turn on my clock radio, finding a station that plays quiet music, that Dibs finally settles down.

CHAPTER 9

Noisy Morning

SHAKE, SHAKE, SHAKE.

Shake, shake, shake.

I open my eyes. Blurry Nicholas is staring over me, shaking my shoulder.

"Becket, get up!" says Nicholas. "I need your help! Hurry!"

I sit up and reach for my glasses on the bedside table. When I put them on, I see that Dibs must have jumped off my bed while I was sleeping. He is all curled up in his crate, his paw resting on Exo. He and Bexo are my oldest stuffies, twin penguins that I got for a birthday so long ago, I can't remember it. I bet Dibs picked Exo for his worn-in smell. "Where did the sun go?"

"It hasn't come up yet! I need you in my room!" Nicholas sounds pretty panicked.

"Okay, okay!"

Nicholas and Dibs follow me down the hall. Nicholas stops in the doorway. He won't go in.

"What will I find in there?"

"Given did it!" Nicholas starts hopping from one foot to the other.

Did what? I tiptoe into the room.

It is very tidy. Nicholas has a rule about his room: If it's smaller than a grapefruit, he puts it in his closet.

I spy something on the floor that is smaller than a grapefruit, or a lemon, or even a lime. It is nestled between Nicholas's fluffy-cat bedroom slippers.

Yipes! It's a dead mouse!

Given is hanging out on the windowsill. Her amber eyes are half-closed, and her tiger tail flicks slowly.

I did that, her proud cat self seems to say. Then she jumps off the sill and disappears under Nicholas's bed.

"I got this, Nicholas," I say over my shoulder. "Looks like Given wanted to give you breakfast. She probably brought the mouse into your room specially. It's gross—but sweet of her, right?"

"Mostly gross, and also scary, and then gross again!" says Nicholas. "Take it out of my room, Becket! I can't go back until it's gone."

"Give me five minutes."

Dibs and Nicholas follow me downstairs. In the kitchen, under the sink, I find a pair of rubber gloves and one of Given's litter bags. We troop back upstairs to Nicholas's room. I scoop up the breakfast mouse, then we all run downstairs again.

Dibs gallops outside with me while Nicholas watches from the window.

I drop the bag of mouse into the outside garbage. I feel bad for Given. Her cat brain thought she'd caught Nicholas a scrumptious morning treat.

The sun is just breaking its yolky gold over the fields. Since I'm already here, I figure I might as well get going on morning chores, collecting eggs from the henhouse and feeding and brushing Pickle and Chew.

Dibs never leaves my side. When I don't let him into the henhouse with me, he starts to howl.

"Stop it, Dibs," I yell out. "You'll scare the

chickens!" I leave the henhouse and try to comfort him. The results aren't so good. Dibs yowls, I go out, soothe him, go in. Dibs yowls again. I go out again. It's like he's yowling because he knows I'll come. I hum a tune, which calms him down a bit, but it still takes forever to collect the eggs.

Dibs sticks close by me as I carry the eggs to the Farm Store mudroom. I wave to Gran, who is already opening up for the morning rush—the store is an excellent pit stop for a cup of strong, hot coffee and a cider doughnut. "Dibs is the new family alarm clock," she says as she takes my basket. "Better than a rooster."

"Given is an even better alarm clock." I tell her about the mouse.

"You can take a cat out of the wild, but you can't take the wild out of a cat."

"What about the dog?"

"Dibs leads with his heart," says Gran. "He needs to get used to routines. Don't let him in the barn when you're there with Pickle and Chew. He might scare them."

I haul Dibs into the kitchen before I go up to the barn, but the whole time I'm feeding Pickle and Chew, I can hear that dog howling his lungs out. When I come back inside, Dibs has made a puddle on the kitchen floor.

"You'll need to clean that up," says Mom, and I go straight to it. "And it's your day to set the table."

"Sorry. He's been upset all morning—eeeyuck!" Doggy pee has seeped through the paper towels onto my hands. "I've been babysitting animals since I got up, and I'm still not dressed for school." I wash my hands, then rush around the table, setting forks and plates.

"Better hurry," says Dad. "I'm making egg-in-a-baskets."

My favorite! Egg-in-a-basket is just egg and toast, but the trick up its sleeve is that it's stuck together. Dad cuts a small hole in the middle of a piece of bread, then fries the egg and bread into buttery, bonded deliciousness.

Meantime, Caroline has joined us to make the fruit salad. She slices apples and bananas. Given darts past and settles on the magazine basket. Dibs scrabbles around the table, excited by all the activity.

"Don't let that dog scrape up my floors!" Dad says.

Dad's voice must have some kind of effect, because Dibs whimpers and lies down under a chair. So Dad comes over and gives Dibs a nice long scratch behind the ears. "I'm your friend, promise, bud," he says quietly.

Nicholas is the last one into the kitchen. He has to hurry to unload the dishwasher, which is his morning chore, before we all sit to breakfast.

But where's Dibs? Not here. I run up to my bedroom to see that he's in his crate, chewing the face off of poor old Exo.

"Dibs!" I cry. "What did Exo do to deserve this?"

Dibs barks an answer at me in his secret dog language.

"Not good enough." I put all my stuffed penguins up on my highest shelf. Exo was no spring chicken of a penguin to begin with, and now he is pretty messed up, with some of his pellets spilling out of his neck.

By the time I'm downstairs again, I've got almost no time to eat. "This is the longest morning," I say. "But also the shortest breakfast morning."

"Let's bring Dibs's crate downstairs and keep him in it while we're gone today," says Mom. "Gran can let him out in the backyard at lunchtime."

One more trip upstairs.

Once I've crated Dibs, I kneel down. "You got this, right, Dibs? You just need to stay quiet and calm, and not scratch or chew or yowl, got it?"

Dibs gives me his best *Sure thing* face. But now I have to lock the crate, and last night I didn't. I have a feeling I've confused him. This pet-training stuff is really hard. I want Dibs to feel happy and comfortable here, and I know I also have to teach him some rules, but I don't like to be too firm, since he's so shy and worried. My heart tugs to see him looking sad, even as I have to walk away.

And, of course, no sooner am I out the door than Dibs starts howling like we never even had our heart-to-heart.

CHAPTER 10

The Bedazzling Branches

"LOOK, BECKET! THE WHOLE SCHOOL IS talking about your wonderful cat, and the Fluff and Puff," says Ms. Lemons, our art teacher. She's on the school's website, looking at all the activities for

the Pumpkin Patch. Caroline's photo of Given is the center picture.

"My sister took that photo," I tell Ms. Lemons proudly.

Ms. Lemons reads the caption: "'Given one's best—at the Fluff and Puff Pet Spa! Photo by Caroline Branch. Please share, adapt, and attribute this image.'"

Ms. Lemons clicks Given's face, and a pop-up message reads:

> Fluff and Puff is a full-service spa! We offer a premium bath with a cream rinse, blow-dry, and style flair. Click the Calendoodle board to schedule your time slot.

"Isn't the word 'Calendoodle' a perfect way to schedule a pet bath?" I say. "It sounds just like a dog breed!"

"It really does! You know what? I'm going to choose a time for my chug,

Mango Lemons, right now," says Ms. Lemons. "He's a pug-Chihuahua mix."

I applaud. "Hooray!" Ms. Lemons is cool like that. Back in September, when school started and I was trying to figure out how to draw animal tails, Ms. Lemons showed me, using a whole lunch period to sit with me at the art table and sketch.

Now I'm pretty good at tails—even stringy ones, which are the hardest.

"See you at the Fluff and Puff," she says once Mango is signed up.

"I'll be there," I say. "And so will Given."

"It's a whole celebrity family," says Ms. Lemons.

A whole celebrity family? I like that!

In the cafeteria, Mr. Peebles, our head lunch person, has printed Given's photo. He's also made a couple of changes, photoshopping in a Thanksgiving table and using a new caption: WE'RE GIVEN THANKS FOR OUR CAN DRIVE!

"What can I say? I'm a total cat person," Mr. Peebles explains when we see his poster at lunchtime. "Great shot, Caroline," he calls across the cafeteria, where Caroline is sitting with Mai and Daisy. His hands make that olden-days motion for snapping a picture.

Caroline nods and looks pleased.

"Just wait till she takes photos of my dog, Dibs," I tell Mr. Peebles. "You'll be a total dog person, too, when you see him."

"I'm already a dog person," says Mr. Peebles. "In fact, I just used the Calendoodle to sign up my beagle, Otis Peebles, for the Fluff and Puff."

GET A *PAWS-ITIVE* CHARGE OUT OF SCIENCE!

That afternoon, we come into the science room to find *another* poster of Given! This time, Given has been photoshopped wearing a lab coat and holding a beaker, and Ms. Kandila has come up with her own caption: GET A PAWS-ITIVE CHARGE OUT OF SCIENCE!

"Given's face brightens a science room better than a dozen glass beakers," says Ms. Kandila. "Caroline is such a talented photographer."

"Everyone in my family is talented," I say proudly. "Nicholas is good at cello, and I'm good at drawing, see?" I pull out my notebook to show her. Luckily, I did some sketches on the margins of my math homework.

"Wow," says Ms. Kandila. "Maybe you should be known as the Bedazzling Branches!"

The Bedazzling Branches! I like that! We really are celebrities!

When Nicholas and I are outside the school waiting for Dad to pick us up, a few sixth graders come up to us. "You're Given's family, right?" asks a girl. "Your cat's like a meme now."

"Yep! That's our cat!" I shout as Nicholas scuffs his sneaker at the ground. "We're getting to be a known family. Some people call us the Bedazzling Branches!"

"Becket." Nicholas looks at me. "We're not called that."

"Ms. Kandila and I call us that! It's our family nickname."

"It's not. Stop saying it."

"But Given really *is* famous."

"I know." Nicholas looks deflated. "It's like she belongs to the whole school."

Just then, Travis saunters by on the way to his bus and calls, "Hey, Nicholas—does your famous cat know you're a kickball crybaby?"

"Hey, Travis," I call. "Remember that time we asked for your opinion about anything? Me neither!" I check to see if Nicholas thinks that's a good one, but his face is a blank.

"You should see if Caroline can photoshop you a better personality, Becket!" calls Travis.

"Didn't mean to push your buttons, Travis—I was looking for 'mute'!"

Travis gives me one last sour face and darts away to his bus.

I am breathing hard. "There's a reason Travis's best friend is a SuperSquid," I say to Nicholas.

"Becket, I wish you wouldn't get into it with Travis," says Nicholas.

"Hey, when it comes to my twin, I feel protective."

"I know, but"—Nicholas has taken out his happy-face stress ball, which he uses whenever I've hidden his fidget spinner—"sometimes you and Travis can remind me of each other."

"What? I'm not anything like Travis! I'm just taking care of you!"

"Yeah, but"—Nicholas shrugs—"you both are kind of looking for attention, and you're both kind of know-it-alls."

"Actually, attention finds me, whether I'm

looking for it or not," I assure him. "Also, I'm nothing like Travis. Not even one tiny speck!"

Nicholas just squeezes his stress ball and says nothing.

CHAPTER 11

Animal Circus

"GIVEN'S SO SASSY!" exclaims Mai when she and Daisy are over later in the week. Zane is here, too. Everyone wants to spend time with our famous cat, who is giving head-boops to any hand that reaches out to pet her.

"Did you see that Mr. Culpepper made a sign of Given for his music room?" says Daisy. "The caption is 'Don't stop me-ow!'"

"Saw that!" says Caroline. "My photo turned Given into a star. I think it's because of the balanced composition." She is flipping through one of Gran's *National Geographic* magazines, studying the nature and animal photos. Lately, Caroline has a lot to say about photography. She loves talking about lights and darks, or warm and cool tones.

"Soon it will be Dibsie's turn to bedazzle," I say. Dibs is curled up in his saucer, not wanting to bedazzle anybody, and I am sketching him. I'm working very hard on his asparagus tail. Maybe if I capture him with extra cuteness, Ms. Lemons will put my sketch on her gallery wall.

Then Dibs could be as famous as Given! Caroline leans over with her phone for a pic of Dibs, but when I ask to see it, he just looks like a scraggly-tailed pillow. I scroll through Caroline's phone photos to check if she's captured any better Dibs poses.

Nope, nope, nope.

Caroline tried, but Dibs is either a blurry bounce or a penny-colored lump. He doesn't like to look into the camera, either.

"Photos don't do him justice," says Caroline. "He's all about real life."

Maybe so. "I'll find a way to make you a star, Dibsie," I tell him, sketching some extra flourish into the asparagus.

So many people are over that Dad decides to make pizza. "Play-date pizza!" he says, and everyone cheers. But Caroline's face is now burrowed into her magazine, and I know she's embarrassed by Dad using the term *play date*.

Dad is serious about his pizza. He rolls his own dough, and we get our mozzarella from Jayne's Dairy, just down the road. Buying local is good for the environment, because the cheese is not coming in after a long-distance truck trip. Also, the basil is from our garden.

"C'mon, Dibs." I close my sketchbook, give a little whistle, and slice off a chunk of mozzarella before I go outside, where Zane is running all around with Given.

"Given can chase a ball!" Zane says to me. "Can Dibs?"

"Working on it," I say as Dibs and I settle on the bottom porch step. I pull some mozzarella from my slice and toss it up in the air. Dibs catches it in his mouth like a seal. I take a bite for myself. I pull off another chunk.

"Sit?" I coax. Dibs cocks his head and waits.

I ask him to sit a few more times, but when he starts whining, I give up. He gulps the cheese and settles back on top of my feet.

"He needs more training," says Zane.

"Yep," I say sadly.

When the pizza is ready, Dad brings it out to the porch table. Everyone trails him. "Outside pizza has extra zing," I tell Dibs, offering him the tiniest bit of crust. "It's a Beautiful Alert combination of cheese, bread, and fresh air."

"A win," agrees Daisy, pressing on my nose freckle. I like when she does that. It's a secret, sparkly Beautiful Alert whenever I get to hang out with Caroline's friends. It makes me feel like I could almost be mistaken for a seventh grader.

"Look what I taught the celebri-cat," says Mai. "Watch this!" She crouches down on the lawn in front of Given. "Shake hands?"

Immediately, Given offers a paw.

Wow! We all give Given a round of applause.

"Given is amazing," says Caroline. "She even

shakes paws! Why isn't Nicholas here to see any of this?"

"He must smell that tomato sauce," says Dad.

"He's upstairs," says Zane. "He told me he needed peace over pizza."

Dibs and I go looking. Upstairs, Nicholas is lying down in the empty bathtub. He's fully dressed, with his headphones on and a pillow behind his head.

The empty bathtub is my twin's happy place, and I know he is listening to his cello lesson, because he's playing invisible notes with his fingers. He takes off his headphones when he sees me.

"Hey," I say, sitting on the edge of the tub. "Why are you hiding in your tub lounge?"

Nicholas sighs. "There's too much fuss around Given. Travis even said it—my cat is too cool for me."

"Travis! Who cares what Travis says?"

"I do, when he's right," says Nicholas. "I think Given is the best cat in the world. She's brave and fun, and everyone loves her. The thing is, I thought my very own cat would belong to me the

most. I imagined her in my room, watching me do homework. But Given thrives on being with lots of people. She doesn't want to miss out on anything."

I look down at Dibs. "Well, I thought I'd have  a friendly dog who'd play with everybody," I admit. "But Dibs doesn't want to make friends with anyone else. He's shyer and more skittish than I imagined, and he's hard to train, too."

As if he knows we're talking about him, Dibs starts thumping his tail. His eyes are warm and sweet like cocoa. Oh, Dibs! My heart hurts with love for him.

"At least you don't understand Dibs any better than I get Given," says Nicholas.

What? No! Of course I understand Dibs!

Don't I?

Do I?

Animals come naturally to me. After all, I'm the one who changes Pickle and Chew's straw bedding, sweeps out their stable, and keeps their salt lick clean. I'm the one who waters the hens' water trough, scooping out bugs, and who soaps the floors once a week to make sure there's not one bit of mold or mildew. I'm really good at my animal chores.

But when it comes to my dog, maybe I *haven't* totally figured him out.

Maybe Nicholas is right.

After all, while trying new recipes comes naturally to Dad, he treasures his cookbook shelf and he's always listening to Gran's tips. Caroline's great at photos, but she spends most of her time looking at other people's pictures for inspiration and examples.

And it's not like Nicholas woke up knowing how to play his cello, Clive. He takes lessons after school, and he's always listening to concerts.

Also, when I knew I was bad at sketching tails, I got help from Ms. Lemons.

So maybe, *maybe* . . . I could use a hand with Dibs.

CHAPTER 12

All Together Now

THE NEXT MORNING, I'M CHANGING INTO MY COVERALLS TO go collect eggs when, from my bedroom window, I see Caroline carrying a straw basket and walking down the path to the henhouse.

That's strange. Gathering eggs is not Caroline's morning chore—it's mine.

After I let Dibs out for his business, he does his sniffing and circles, and then he wants to come with me to feed the chickens. I take him into the kitchen instead.

"Stay," I command. But then he yowls. I back away. He keeps yowling.

So I return, and hug him.

I feel so bad for him that I just don't know what to do.

Dibs is still yowling like an opera star when I go outside and shut the kitchen door. I open it. Just one more hug. "Dibs, I love you, but you take up too much of my time," I tell him. "You are my hardest chore by far."

Dad, who's making egg-and-cheese biscuits in the kitchen, says I should feed Dibs before I head for the hens. "Pro tip: Get that dog on an early breakfast schedule, and he won't yowl nearly so much."

So I feed Dibs, which calms him

down. The morning is cold enough for one more layer, and Dad says he doesn't mind if I take his barn jacket. It's olive green with a flannel lining, and it falls to my knees. I button it up and it's like a Dad hug.

Outside, there's a spicy-woodsmoke and crisp-apple-y scent in the air. It's a Beautiful Alert shout for my nose.

In the henhouse, Caroline crouches by the nest box, where Wilma and Betty, our Rhode Island Reds, are roosting. Caroline's face is serious. When I check on her basket, there's only one egg—and I'd bet my last banana she took it from an empty nest, and not a sitting hen.

I scooch down next to her as I place my finger on my lips. Then, without speaking, I show her how to slide a hand carefully underneath Wilma's fluffy feathers to her undercarriage.

I withdraw an egg. Presto!

Caroline makes a face. "It seems so rude!" she whispers.

"Not to me. I'm friends with hens," I say. "But why are you here?"

"Because of the pet spa." Worry makes her eyes look sad. "I keep imagining Sunday in a nervous way. Mai and Daisy won't like if I'm unhelpful with the dogs."

"You should tell Mai straight up that you don't want to do the animals part. Also, handling the money isn't as simple as they think. Gran taught you how to make change and use the credit card machine at the store."

"I guess." Caroline's cheeks flush as her hands grip the egg basket. "What's wrong with me? I live on a farm, and both our parents are vets!"

"You've just got to make people listen up about the things you're good at," I say. "And stop caring about what you can't do. That's my forever advice! Now, look and learn."

Caroline watches me collect the rest of the eggs.

Every time I have to scoop under a hen, I can tell that it ruffles Caroline's feathers.

As we come into the kitchen, Dad's got breakfast ready and Nicholas has set the table. But Mom is on the phone, pacing back and forth, with what turns out to be troubling news. Principal Vera's border collie, Rosie, might have broken her leg.

"Principal Vera, as in the middle school principal?" asks Caroline.

Mom nods. "The farm is on the way to Boggs Hollow. If we leave now, I can splint Rosie's leg before I drop you all off at school."

Vet emergencies don't happen often, but when they do, we all pitch in. Sometimes, it means making our own dinners, if Mom and Dad are in a surgery. Sometimes, it means being stuck at the clinic while Mom and Dad tend to a patient. This time, it means we grab our breakfasts to go, and we're all in the car in less than a minute. Dad's following behind with Mom's vet bag, which she forgot.

When Nicholas comes running out last—biscuit sandwich in hand—sneaky little Dibs slips outside along with him. Dibs is yowling away.

Dad just scoops up Dibs as Mom pops out of the car. Dad gives her a little kiss on the cheek as he hands her the vet bag.

"Unbreak a leg," he says as Nicholas slides in next to me.

"Turn the kitchen radio on for Dibs," I shout out the window, and we're off.

"WHEN YOU SAID you'd be here right away, you meant it!" Principal Vera looks relieved when she opens the front door of her house. "My goodness, it's the whole crew."

"We might be a one-car family with two working parents and three kids," says Mom. "But we know how to move as a unit if we need to."

"I'll say." Principal Vera beams. "Rosie's just in here. She hurt her leg jumping over the rail fence." She looks over at us. "You're more than welcome to join my husband and Piper. They're around back, herding the sheep from the front pasture into the back pen. Without Rosie, they'll need all the help they can get."

"That sounds pretty fun!" I say. I did not know when I woke up this morning there'd be some sheep herding slipped inside my day!

Nicholas, Caroline, and I run over to the field while Mom takes a look at Rosie's leg.

"Piper is trying, but she's still a puppy. Rosie is still teaching her the ropes," says Mr. Vera as he points out the stumpy-legged corgi running in circles around and nosing at the huddles of sheep. "I've got about half of them herded.

Just help me run along the edges. They'll get the picture." Mr. Vera's cheeks and the tips of his ears are as red as a boiled hot dog! He looks like he's already been huffing and puffing out here for a while.

It's cold and bright here in the Veras' field, and the air smells like pasture. Caroline moves carefully at the very outside hem of the herd, mostly keeping away from the sheep while still managing to be, technically, on the field. Nicholas runs along the sides, near the stragglers. But I move in close. I'm a sheepdog! I *urf* at the sheep, listening to my voice spread wide over the entire meadow, as I reach out my hands to brush against their woolly backs.

They *baaaaaa* and *baaaaaa* whenever Piper nips their legs.

What a fun chore this is turning out to be!

It takes effort, but eventually we get the last sheep penned.

Then Mom comes outside with Principal Vera, who signals a thumbs-up.

"Thanks, kids," says Mr. Vera as he walks over to the car with us. "Rosie thanks you, too."

"And me too," says Principal Vera. "All this cooperation!"

"We have a saying in our house: 'Many Branches, one tree,'" says Mom.

"Well, I feel like I've just seen the Branch family's superpower!" says Principal Vera. "See you in school, Super Branches."

Super Branches! I like that! We climb back into the car and head to school. "I guess you and Dad have got us kids all pretty well trained, don't you, Mom?" I ask as we drive away.

"'Trained' is probably not the word we'd use," says Mom. "I think of us more as all pulling together. Because we're all on the same team, right?" She smiles as she gets a glimpse of me through the rearview mirror.

"Team Super Branch?"

"Team Family," she answers.

CHAPTER 13

Needers and Weeders

AFTER SCHOOL, THE FIRST THING I DO IS MAKE A COUPLE OF additions to the chore board, squeezing two extra names above Caroline's. I'm a Branch who's going out on a limb, but I think this plan might work best.

Then I take Dibs outside.

"Listen," I tell him. "You're also part of the Super Branches, Dibs. We're all on one team. No special rules for you—not even when you howl, or when you look at me with those melty chocolate eyes. If you're *my* chore, then I'm *your* chore, too. Let's start with Stay."

Dibs doesn't like Stay. He's doesn't like to watch me backing away from him. We work on it. When I see Dad walking up from the driveway, I signal him to join us.

"Will you help me train Dibs?" I ask. "I want him to start trusting your voice."

"Sure thing," says Dad.

Together, Dad and I work on Stay. We practice Angel's balancing trick, too. Dibs still prefers me to Dad, but he likes the way Dad scratches him under the collar.

"See you this time tomorrow, okay?" I ask Dad. He first

gives me a look like I just told him to go make his bed. But then he answers, "Sure."

"Hey, Becket," calls Nicholas to me from the doorway. "Mom says come inside and weed out stuff in your room to donate to the Pumpkin Patch pop-up thrift shop."

"Did you do it?"

"Yup, but I've got a system," he says. "If I haven't used something for a year, then I don't need it anymore."

That does not sound like the right system for me. "Let's go, Dibs," I say.

Mom is in the upstairs hall. She points to the big cardboard box in front of her. "Weed out things you don't need. The school is doing a pickup tomorrow."

"I'll try," I say. "But I'm more of a needer than a weeder."

Mom smiles. "Here's a trick. If you see something to donate but you're not positive, touch it and think of a reason why it should stay. If you can't, out it goes."

"Okay," I tell her. "Oh, also, you might want to check the chore board? I've made some additions."

Mom looks puzzled, but she says, "I'll be sure to do that, Becket."

My room is a good balance of tidy and messy. My bed is made, but my pajamas drape over my chair like Flat Stanley. My desk always looks like I'm in the middle of a cool art project.

I look through my clothes. Then I go through my sketchbooks and art supplies and stickers and stuffed animals. I know donating is good for the environment, because it keeps the treasures circulating instead of ending up in a landfill. But the problem with *me* donating things is that—I love my stuff! My room is like a scrapbook of my memories jumbled up with my now. It's who I've been and who I am, all mixed up together.

Soon I get tired of not weeding and mostly needing. I lie down on my bed with my penguins. I stretch out my legs and my neck and shoulders. A bunch of penguins together on the ice is called a waddle. I close my eyes and picture myself, solid and steady at the center of my icy waddle of penguins. Something feels just a tick wrong with my ice waddle, but I can't figure out what.

As soon as I hear Mom heading up to the attic, Dibs and I swoop downstairs and outside. Nicholas and Given are in the yard, running back and forth. Then Dibs and Given start chasing each other, so Nicholas and I lie on our backs and stare up at the sky, just like we've been doing since we first learned how to run around and collapse from games.

Eventually Dibs and Given lie down next to us.

We are like a double set of twins. I wish Caroline could snap this picture. Everyone at school would be so astounded to see the Bedazzling Branches with their animal twins.

"The best thing about being twins is that we never need to prove to anybody how lucky we are," says Nicholas. "Being twins just *is*."

This has got to be the most opposite thought in the world from the one I was having. But it also reminds me that my twin and I are every bit as bedazzlingly different as we are remarkably alike. I close my eyes as I slip this excellent moment into my memory scrapbook.

CHAPTER 14

Family Fortune

I FEED DIBS DINNER RIGHT ON SCHEDULE. WHEN HE'S DONE, we stay in the kitchen, practicing his nose-balancing trick while Mom and Dad make lasagna. By the time Caroline and Nicholas come downstairs, it's in the oven.

"Sometimes I would love to be a dog. But *not* when I'm having goopy, gloppy, cheesy lasagna while Dibs just gets a bowl of dry kibble," I say. In answer, Dibs burps. I toss the ball, and he misses again. "Lasagna is like if the word 'wow' was food!

All I want to say when I eat lasagna is, 'Wow, wow, WOW!'"

"'Wow' is exactly what I said when I looked at the chore board and noticed Dad's and my names," says Mom. "Plus it looks like we've got some new chores."

Caroline has started chopping carrots for the salad, while Nicholas is opening a tin of cat food. Now they both look over at the board to see my

additions. Caroline laughs. "Why are Mom and Dad helping you train Dibs every day?"

"Because we all need to pull together as a unit," I

explain. "I need help, and Dibs deserves help. After all, he's a working member of the Branch family."

"I'm game," says Mom.

"I like seeing my name on the chore board," says Dad. "Takes me back."

Mom reaches in the cupboard and pulls out a dish. "This takes me back, too. But not in a good way."

"It's Gran's Kermit serving dish," I say.

"I think he's going into the Pumpkin Patch donations pile," says Mom.

"Not Kermit," says Dad, who has started to mix up the salad dressing. "He's a keeper."

"No. Weed him out," says Nicholas. He sets down Given's bowl and goes to wash his hands at the sink. "Kermit always makes me feel like we're eating from a frog's insides."

"Agree. Let's weed him," says Caroline. "Gran hasn't used Kermit for a long time."

"But she might still want him," I say. "I vote Kermit stays."

"I second Becket," says Dad. "Maybe we could

pop some ferns in Kermit, turn him into a planter, and call him Fern-it?"

"Uh-oh, Dad joke alert," says Caroline.

"Gran always says that anything she's left in the big house is ours," says Nicholas. "That means 'bye, Kermit.'"

"I second Nicholas," says Caroline.

"Three votes against two," says Mom. "That's a 'bye, Kermit' confirm it."

"Gran isn't here to vote," I remind everyone. "It's three against three."

"That is not a 'bye, Kermit' permit," says Dad.

"Here," says Mom, handing me Kermit. "Go ask Gran herself."

"Practice is over for now," I tell Dibs, pocketing the ball.

Dibs follows me. First I check Branch's Farm Store, but Gran isn't there, or in her upstairs apartment. Outside again, I see a light from the pony barn. Our pony barn doesn't have any ponies, but it's where we keep summer stuff, like our lawn mower and porch cushions and, most recently, boxes for the pop-up.

There's Gran. She has opened a couple of boxes. Strewn on the barnwood floor are stacks of chipped plates and mugs, an electric fan, and some paintings by Dad from when he took a watercolor class and learned that he did not have any talent whatsoever for painting.

"Mom's wondering if you still want this," I say, holding up Kermit.

"Aw, Kermit," she says. "Let's not give away that cutie! And since you're here now, help me find my recipe box." Gran is using her pie-cutting knife to split the tape on another carton top. "It's full of old family photos."

"Um, Gran. I think Mom will want us to repack everything."

But Gran just opens the carton and squeaks with joy. "My knitting basket!"

"My old coveralls!" I say. I pull them out of a box of clothes that Mom ended up weeding for

me. They are too short now, but I had so many Beautiful Alerts wearing them. They are as soft as a daydream. I also find my light-up caterpillar bookends and my lucky cracked jam jar, still full of bottle caps.

"Dinner's ready." I didn't hear Dad come in. He stands in the barn's doorway, looking around. "What's happening here?"

"I'm hunting down my recipe box," says Gran.

Dad stoops to pick up something from Gran's pile. "Simon Sole in Tune!" He clicks the ON switch of a painted wooden fish. Simon's fish lips start to sing "Take Me to the River" as his tail swishes back and forth.

"Still works!" Then Dad sets down Simon and looks in the closest box. "My casual Fridays Hawaiian shirt! My 'Best Dad Ever' mug!"

Now I look in the box. Mr. Fancypants's bowl! And down at the bottom, smelling in the best way possible like old milk and dish rags—Bexo? I squeeze him so hard that I think I hear him squeak. "That's why my waddle felt light. You weren't on it."

"What is happening here?"

We all freeze in place. It's Mom's shadow in the doorway now. She's as stiff as a reed, with her arms crossed over her chest. Nobody wants to be the first to answer.

"I need to keep Simon, and my mug," says Dad quietly.

"I need Kermit, and my recipe box," says Gran as she starts digging again.

"And I need Bexo," I say. "And maybe my old coveralls?"

"Eureka!" Gran holds up a red-and-white-checked metal box with a handle. "I knew I'd find it!"

Mom's lips are thinned out. I can feel that she wants to say many things, but the words she ends up using are, "Lasagna's waiting, folks. And you don't need to check the chore board to know we'll all need to repack after dinner."

CHAPTER 15

Twins through Time

GRAN TRANSFERS THE LASAGNA FROM THE PAN INTO KERMIT. She cuts the cheesy pasta into squares, like bake-sale brownies.

The squares are so slippery they're hard to ladle out. And the more I think that the lasagna is cooked frog, the less I want to eat.

Maybe I should have voted to weed Kermit, after all.

After dinner, we split chores. Mom and Dad head back to the barn to repack the boxes while the rest of us clean up. Dibs and Given

chase each other around and around the living room.

"Is Given teaching Dibs how to bat paws like a cat?" asks Nicholas.

"I think so. Dibs is definitely teaching Given how to nip like a dog," I say.

Gran is at the kitchen table. She has opened her recipe box. Her expression is soft and faraway. Quietly, Caroline comes up with her phone to take pictures of Gran.

"I'm capturing a mood," Caroline whispers.

Gran looks up. "Kids, come look at some family photographs."

We all gather around. Some of them are on flimsy paper that is curling up at the edges. Others are on thick film as stiff as cardboard. A few others are on flat pieces of tin. Gran knows who all the strangers are. It's hard to think of Gran being part of any family except ours.

"Here's my grandmother, Maxine, with her twin brother," says Gran, picking up a large metal square. "Twins run in the family." She hands me the photograph. It's a boy and girl, sitting on a stiff-backed sofa. The bottom of the photo says BEALES PHOTOGRAPHIC STUDIO, 1889. "Maxine is your great-great-grandmother, and her brother is your great-great-great-uncle Maxwell. They were only eleven here."

"That's pretty far back," I say.

"I'll say! But I go pretty far back, too," says Gran. "I only remember my grandmother with white hair and wrinkles. Look how young she is here!"

Maxine has a pouf of hair like a bread roll on top of her head. Her boots are scuffed, like she'd been on an adventure. Maxwell's boots are scuffed, too—were they playing one of those olden-days games, like Hoop and Stick? You can tell they are brother and sister by their matching square foreheads and longish noses.

"What were they like?" I ask.

Gran smiles. "Maxine and Maxwell got up to some hijinks. Once, they hid a mouse in their grandmother's bed!"

Nicholas shivers. "What if Given does that to me?"

"No." I shake my head. "Given is only trying out ways to make your room cozy and homey. Not creepy and scary."

"Finding dead mice is not cozy and homey," says Nicholas.

"She knows that now."

As if she hears her name, Given jumps up and struts along the back of Nicholas's chair. When he holds up his hand, she boops it with her head.

"Do you think she picked my chair specially?"

asks Nicholas. "Do you think she knows I'm her main person?"

"Of course," Gran, Caroline, and I say all together.

But privately, I think Given could have picked anyone's chair for a strut.

Later, when I go upstairs to brush my teeth, Nicholas is already in bed playing Solitaire, a card game Gran taught us. His face is serious.

"What's wrong?" I ask.

He sighs. "I always hope Given will come sleep in my room. But she never does. So I put her sleep saucer downstairs again. It's not like I can train her, either."

"But that's the cool part about Given," I tell him. "You never know what she'll do next. She hasn't picked her sleep spot yet."

"I can't train her to do anything. Not like how you train Dibs," says Nicholas.

"Dibs is very time-consuming," I say.

Nicholas smiles. "Given takes care of herself," he says. "I like that about her."

"And I like that Dibs needs my help," I say. "Want to play Crazy Eights?"

"Yes!" says Nicholas.

After two rounds of Crazy Eights and one hand of Spit, I'm sleepy, so I say goodnight to Nicholas and head to my bedroom.

I whistle softly for Dibs, who comes bounding right up. Once he's settled in his crate, I'm about to turn off my bedside table lamp when I hear a knock on my door.

"Come in!"

Caroline? Now that's a first! She looks a little bit uncertain.

I smile. "What's up?"

"Can I join you tomorrow to help feed Pickle and Chew?" she asks.

"Of course!"

Caroline's face softens. "Thanks," she says. "I'm scared of that donkey."

"Pickle's just like a dog, but bigger."

She wrinkles her nose. "I'm not sure that makes me feel better." She glances at Dibs's crate, where he is snoring. "How can you sleep with that noise?"

"I like it. It's company. He doesn't need the radio anymore—*that* was noise."

She nods. "I guess you're not lonely since you have Dibs now, but you can always stop by my room and say hi," she says. "In fact, I'd kind of gotten used to your visits." Caroline pats the lump of my feet at the end of my bed. "Sometimes I miss sharing a room with you."

I'm so surprised that all I can say is, "Uh-huh," but after she leaves, I snap off my lamp with a smile in my heart.

CHAPTER 16

Fair in the Air

ON THE SUNDAY MORNING OF OUR VERY FIRST BRANCH family Pumpkin Patch, we are all up with the birds.

"Gonna shine with a little help from my friends," I sing as I do morning chores. Sometimes the right song can coax the sun out.

But this cool, silvery fall day feels good on my cheeks, too.

"I think Given should stay home," says Nicholas as we're getting ready to leave. "It will be too many people. And some of those people are Travis the Terrible and his SuperSquid."

"I'll protect her," I say. "Given's the star of the spa. Everyone will be so excited to see her."

"And if she doesn't like it, we can wait in the car," says Nicholas. I nod in agreement.

"Mai got Given a harness with a clip-on leash," says Caroline.

"Now I've heard it all," says Gran. "A cat on a leash!"

"I just hope Dibs doesn't start chasing Given," says Mom. "Please keep your eyes on your pets, kids. We wouldn't want to lose you, Dibsie." She makes the clicking sound that she, Dad, and I have been working on. We decided that since all of our voices are different, we ought to find sounds that Dibs would understand, no matter who said them.

Dibs hears the clicks and trots over to Mom.

As everyone starts putting on coats and shoes, I make the clicking sound so that Dibs will come over to me. Once Nicholas tucks Given into the cat carrier, we head out.

Gran is already gone, getting a jump start on Branch's Twig, which is her own pop-up version of Branch's Farm Store.

"Stay, Dibs," I command. He stays as still as a statue on the welcome mat. "Now watch this," I tell the others. I open the carrier, and he hops right in.

"Nice work, Team Branch," says Mom.

It's not until we're halfway to school, with the carrier tucked in right beside me, that I can feel Dibs get that same tense weight and muscle stillness I remember from when we first brought him home. Come to think of it, Dibs hasn't been anywhere since he started living here. The only

people he's seen are our family, plus Daisy, Mai, and Zane.

And now I'm about to take him into a whole new environment.

"Everything's gonna be okay, ole boy," I tell him.

In the carrier, very faintly, Dibs whimpers.

THE SCHOOL PARKING lot is almost full. With so many booths and games, I don't know where to put my eyes first.

"Let's check out the pop-up thrift shop!" Dad says. He is already picking up his pace as we walk across the parking lot and onto the sports field.

Dibs is padding beside me, slowly but not too shyly, on his leash, which he is still getting used to. As soon as he sees the crowd, he starts to pant and whine, so I get him in the carrier. Whew! Dibs has put on weight since he's come to live at Blackberry Farm. I heave the carrier higher on my shoulder.

"It's okay, Dibs. It's just people," I tell him. Lots and lots of people.

The pop-up thrift shop is like a tiny outside store. Cardboard tags label the sections as CLOTHES, HOUSEWARES, OUTDOORS, and CURIOSITIES. In the kids' clothes section, my weeded coveralls are hanging on a rack. It hurts my heart to see them not belonging to me anymore. I touch my fingers to the front pocket, where I liked to keep my treasures. These coveralls look so much smaller than the ones I wear now. They kind of seem like a younger version of me.

It was the right idea to say goodbye to them. Now they're ready to be adopted for another kid's adventures.

"Uh-oh." Mom's eyes are following Dad, who is making a beeline straight to the men's clothes section. "Somebody stop him." She sighs. "I think that somebody is me. Bye, kids. I'll come by the pet spa later, to see how you're doing."

Over by the kickball field is a bouncy castle, a bouncy rocket, and a bouncy slide—and all of them have lots of bouncers already. It looks like so much fun!

"Food first, or bouncing?" asks Caroline, checking her watch. "We have half an hour before the first Calendoodle slot." Mai and Daisy are over there already, setting up the Fluff and Puff, since we three are in charge of cleanup. So we've got a little time.

"Bouncing," I say at the same time that Nicholas says, "Food."

Caroline doesn't want to bounce. She holds on to Dibs's carrier while I go get my bounce on. I get tickets for the castle, the rocket, *and* the slide, and when I meet up with Caroline and Nicholas at the frozen custard stand my stomach feels upside-down. But frozen custard takes care of that. There's also a cotton candy cart, a caramel apple and hot cocoa bar, a pretzel station, a Sprinkle Dee-Dee Bakery pop-up, and a panini booth that is pressing grilled cheeses as fast as people can order them.

"I spy Gran," says Nicholas.

We all run over. Of all the stalls at the Pumpkin Patch, Branch's Twig is—in my opinion—the sweetest! It's got that homemade farmy feel. Gran has stocked up on her lemon loaves, banana breads, and twist-tied bags of oat-and-honey granola, plus jars of Branch's You Are My Sunshine Apple Butter and Branch's Spicy Zucchini Relish.

"I'm already sold out of the butter and yogurt," says Gran.

Eww! Yogurt is the one dairy item I never like. The taste reminds me of sweaty ice cream. Just thinking about it makes me squirm.

"Maybe I should help you out here instead, Gran," says Caroline, checking her watch.

Just then, a sharp whistle cuts the air. "Branches! It's time!" Mai waves.

The Fluff and Puff is set up on the shady patio with picnic tables, right outside the middle school cafeteria. We got this spot because we needed running water and a power outlet.

Daisy, Frieda, and Mai have put out the tub. They're using one of the picnic tables for the towels, brushes and combs, and cute accessories.

But why is *Travis* here?

"My cousin Mai told me I can help," says Travis. "I love water!"

"You two are *cousins*?" I splutter.

Mai nods. She looks a little bit embarrassed. I wouldn't brag about it, either, if Travis were my cousin. "We've got an extra apron for him," says Mai. "They were donated by Schneckenburgers'." She is already wearing one. It's pretty adorable, with a big blue paw print on the pocket.

"Travis SuperSquid-ed Nicholas's and my birthday cake," I say.

"He didn't bring his squid today," says Mai. "We've all got our strengths, I guess—and Travis's strength is, um, water. Today you'll use your powers for good, right, Travis?"

"Yep," says Travis.

"My strength is avoiding Travis," mutters Nicholas. "Or it *was*, anyway."

Caroline casts a longing look back over her shoulder at Branch's Twig, but Mai's already got the apron tied around her.

When Caroline picks up the metal cash box, Mai and Daisy trade a knowing glance.

"Caroline," says Mai. "Don't you want to take off your nails?"

"Oh," says Caroline. She bites her lip.

"How else are you going to help wash the pets?" asks Daisy.

"After all," says Mai, "we've got a lot of work to do. We need to make sure the shampoos don't go into overtime, we need to keep the water fresh—and someone always has got to be working the cash box. Everyone shares the work, okay?"

"For sure." Caroline nods, but her cheeks are flushed. "And I can take the pictures, too. I'm ready for anything." She is already peeling off her stick-on nails. When she glances over at me nervously, all I see is the sister who has been working with Pickle and Chew and the hens all week. If I'm naturally easy around animals, Caroline is just as naturally uneasy, but she has really tried her best.

"You got this," I tell her in a quiet voice.

"Hey, everybody!" Coach Valentine waves as he runs up. He's our assigned grown-up to help out with the spa. For a while, the attention is off Caroline as we all learn how to hook up and run the hose. We fill the metal tub with warm, sudsy water before our first pet arrives.

Nicholas is presenting Given to the world. Out of her carrier, in her tiny harness, she is sitting like a queen on top of a picnic table. Her head is up and her tail flicks, as if to say, *Come look at me, everyone!*

Dibs won't leave the carrier. "Come on, Dibs! It's all friends out here," I coax. From inside, I hear the nervous *thump, thump, thump* of his asparagus tail. He's not coming out. He's going to save all his bedazzling for the family. "Okay, then. Stay," I tell him. I keep the crate door open slightly, even though when I check, he's balled up like a pill bug.

"Now you can watch all the other dogs get a good scrub-down," I tell him. "But you can sit out the bath part. That would be a lot for a shy Dibs like you."

Dibs pants his agreement.

"Oro's got the first Calendoodle slot," announces Frieda as she bounds up with Oro, who is wagging his whole hind end in greeting. But it's Given who is the star of the show. A crowd starts gathering around her table like she's a museum display.

"It's the poster cat!"

"The same cat from science!"

"From art class!"

"From music!"

"From the lunchroom!"

Given purrs and struts and poses and preens from all the attention.

As much as I don't want to admit it, water *is* Travis's strength today. He loves to fill the tub, and he doesn't mind getting into the suds and soap as he scrubs down Oro with me. We deliver a sopping-wet Oro to Frieda and Daisy, and Mai and Nicholas turn out to be a great team at the towel-down and hair-dryer station.

Then Travis and I refresh the tub. We won't do a full tub dump because we want to conserve water. Got to use those conservation smarts, especially when our goal is green energy! Travis is not bad when it comes to heavy lifting, and he seems as happy as a pack of puppies to be putting himself to good use.

Mai leaps to the cash box to make change for Mr. Franca while he's asking Caroline to take a couple of photos of Oro getting his neckerchief tied.

Otis Peebles is our next dog, followed by Mango Lemons—two small-sized and easy pets. We divide into two teams to scrub them down, then blow-dry them into fluffy, puffy beauty. Otis also gets a neckerchief, and Mango gets a yellow bow for each ear as Caroline takes photos of everything.

"Must be nice," says Daisy, "being mostly the photographer. That's the fancy work, I guess." She and Mai exchange another look. I know Caroline feels embarrassed, but she probably doesn't want me making excuses for her or saying things like "I can do the work for two!"—which is what I want to say.

Then Mr. Franca comes running back over with Oro, and he's waving a couple of bills. "Hey there, Mai—I think you might have given me the wrong change," he says.

"Dang, I'm sorry! Hang on a minute," says Mai as she takes money from Mr. Peebles. At this moment, Oro decides it would be fun to use his teeth to pull Mango's bow.

"Let's just figure this out real quick," says Mr. Franca, "so I can get Oro away from the other dogs."

"Caroline!" shouts Mai. "You wanted to do the money part—help me out?"

"Wait a sec," says Ms. Lemons. "Take just one more photo, Caroline. But first, I need to redo Mango's bow."

"No problem," Caroline says to Ms. Lemons. "I'll be right there!" she calls to Mai, just as Mrs. Schneckenburger strolls over with her dog, Bijoux.

"I brought my own shampoo!" she says, holding up a tiny pink bottle. "And careful—Bijoux hates water. Also, I don't have cash. Do you have a mobile credit card machine? And may I pay now?"

"Actually, I've got to get my change first," says Mr. Franca.

"Then I'm next," says Ms. Lemons. "Also, I've brought my bag of loose change. I'm planning to spend it all at the Pumpkin Patch!"

"I can pay right this second, though, if you have a mobile machine," says Mrs. Schneckenburger.

"Yes, but I was here first," says Mr. Franca. "Oh, and Caroline—I want you to take a photo with me and Daisy."

"We do have a mobile machine," Mai says to Mrs. Schneckenburger. "But I don't know, exactly, um, how to work it. Caroline?" She sounds flustered. "Caroline, hurry!"

"Coming," says Caroline, quickly snapping some pictures of the Francas with Oro, then some more pictures of Mango, before swooping in to take charge of the money. Mai looks grateful to be released from duty as Caroline expertly corrects Mr. Franca's change, handles Mrs. Schneckenburger's card, and starts counting out the stacks of Ms. Lemon's dimes and quarters.

"Thanks, Caroline," murmurs Mai. "Every time I closed my eyes and tried to do the pluses and take-aways, the numbers kept jumbling up! It got me panicking. I think you'd better take over the money full-time!"

"No problem," says Caroline, and now it's our turn to trade a knowing look.

"Yoo-hoo!" It's Principal Vera with a whole other problem to solve. "Anyone know how to wash a sheepdog with a leg in a splint?"

CHAPTER 17

Suds and Selfies

"ROSIE!" I EXCLAIM. WE ARE ALL A BIT STARTLED TO SEE HER.

Rosie is, by far, the mud-crustiest dog who has shown up here today.

"That's not a dog for the tub," declares Daisy.

"All hands on deck," says Mai. "We'll do a hose-down."

"Let's wrap her leg in a towel," I add. "We need to keep it dry."

As we get Rosie sudsed, Caroline takes some photos and then shows them to Principal Vera, who bursts out laughing. "You've captured her! That's hilarious!"

We all clamber to see. The bubbles on Rosie's head look sort of like a puffy beret—and in one picture, the way her mouth is open she could be smiling.

"What wonderful images," says Principal Vera, leaning in as Caroline scrolls through some of the photos she's taken today. "Will you email them to me? The photographer is one of the most important jobs at the Pumpkin Patch! It's how we get our message out!"

"Sure," says Caroline. Her face is sunshiny with relief, and I know she can't believe her luck. Caroline turned out to be the star of the Fluff and Puff, and she didn't have to wash or dry one single pet!

But, whew, Rosie is a project! And once she's done, we hardly have a break before Bowser "the

Schnauzer" Brown, then Sherlock McBride, who is a Dalmatian mix, then Radish Crestadoro, a Weimaraner, and then a pair of hounds named Chewy and Chomp Ali come our way. Everyone wants to say hi to Given—people just love it when

they recognize her from the Boggs Hollow website. There's so much going on here at the Fluff and Puff that nobody notices—until suddenly I do, and the hair stands up on my arms and the back of my neck.

Dibs's carrier flap is all the way open. I've been paying so much attention to fluffing and puffing, and Given's bedazzling, that I can't even remember the last time I checked in on Dibs. Was it five minutes ago? Ten? My heart is hammering.

I run to check. Dibs is not in his carrier.

"Dibs!" I shout. I look around. I spin in a circle. But he's nowhere.

CHAPTER 18

Vanished

"DIBS!" I CALL ACROSS THE FIELD. "DIBSIE! DIBS!" I'M A thousand layers of feelings, all at once—frightened, guilty, worried, confused, panicked. I'd left the carrier open only because Dibs has never, ever shown any interest in leaving it unless coaxed.

What a terrible idea that was!

"He couldn't have gone far," says Caroline in her calmest older-sister voice, the voice that can talk Nicholas down from his thunderstorm fears, or break apart a math word problem into easy pieces so that I can solve the equation.

Given, on the picnic table, stares at us and gives a tiny meow.

"Given, where's Dibs?" I ask. I can't shake the feeling that the cat knows something she's not telling.

Given just sits. Tail flicking. Eyes narrowed.

I pick up the chew toy from inside the dog carrier and hold it under Given's nose. "Can you find a scent? Animal instinct! Where did Dibs go?"

"I think . . . maybe." Travis clears his throat. "So, I saw Dibs's nose sticking out of the carrier, and he was panting, and I . . ."

"What?" I pounce over to him and look him in the eye. "What did you do?" I stamp my foot. "Tell me, Travis!"

"I poured a little bit of water on his head," Travis tells me. "Because he looked so hot. He was

just lying there, panting! But then he jumped up."

"So you *saw* him run away?"

"No! I mean—I don't know."

"WATER IS NOT THE ANSWER FOR EVERYTHING, TRAVIS!"

"There's no time to point fingers," says Caroline. "Mai, Daisy, and Travis, you stay here and handle the customers. Becket, Nicholas, and I will start the search. Let's try to find Dibs without getting Mom and Dad involved."

"On it." Nicholas scoops Given into his arms. "We'll go look around by the ticket booth."

"I'm going to check out the food stalls," I say. "Most dogs follow their noses straight to the snacks."

"I'll come with you," says Caroline.

But Dibs is not at any of the snack stations. When we stop by Branch's Twig, and Gran learns Dibs is gone, she closes to help out.

"Dibs won't go far," Gran says, trying to reassure me.

"We don't know where Dibs might go!" I say.

We do a lap, avoiding Mom and Dad, before Caroline and I decide to split up.

"Gran and I'll go over to the games field," she says.

"I'll take the parking lot."

I run around searching until I'm one big ache of worry. I try to think how Dibs thinks. What would I do if I were a dog who got lost at a school? Where would I go? What would feel safe? The school building? I dash to the doors, which are open for the Pumpkin Patch so that people can use the restrooms.

"Has anyone seen a dog with a white star marking?" I ask the small group of people who are waiting outside the restroom doors.

"Nope," says a kid who is sitting on the floor, his back against the wall, chewing on a caramel apple. "And I've been here for a long time."

If you walk into Boggs Hollow Elementary any Monday through Friday, you will see Mrs. Stebbins at the front desk and Mr. Zacchi, our hall monitor, making sure kids keep moving left or right to get to their classrooms. Not today. Today, it's so quiet! As I edge in deeper, past the restrooms and Mrs. Stebbins's desk, and I fork left by habit, because that's where Mr. Dragan's classroom is, I can hear the squeak of my own sneakers and the echo of my breath.

It feels like I'm trespassing at my own school!

I whistle. "Dibs! Dibsie! Come on, boy!"

Nothing.

The art room and the cafeteria, so crowded with kids on a school day, are deserted. So is the library, which is usually thick with whispers and laughing.

I whistle again, louder. "Dibs, are you in here?"

Then I tiptoe into the cafeteria kitchen, where I have never been. All week, there's so much noise from inside here, especially when the doors swing open.

This silence just doesn't feel right—and neither does the fact that I can't smell tomato soup and fish sticks. But Dibs loves the kitchen at home, so maybe. I'm still standing, staring at the rows of cooking pots for clues, when I think I hear someone calling for help.

"Hello? Who's there?" I run back out into the hall. "Anyone?"

Now I don't hear anything. Did I imagine it?

Since nobody is watching me, I figure I might as well sneak a quick minute inside the teacher's lounge across the hall.

I crack open the door. "Dibs?"

There's a coffee urn, some soft old furniture, a bowl that looks like it should have a fish in it but doesn't, and—yum!—a box of iced cookies. I'm halfway to taking a cookie when I think I hear . . . music?

CHAPTER 19

Hide and Peek

I LEAVE THE LOUNGE. MY EARS WERE RIGHT.

Floom, floom, floom! Someone is playing the harp, and whoever it is wants somebody to hear it. And who would be playing music in the music room except for a ghost?

Spooky! But also exciting! I can't remember any of the rules for getting away from a ghost. Are they the same as if you run into a bear?

171

If you see a bear, you're supposed to speak calmly and back away slowly.

But let's face it, if I really saw a bear—or a ghost—I wouldn't be doing either of those things. I'd be running, hard!

"Dibs?" I call.

Floom! answers the harp.

Then it plays something I recognize—one of Nicholas's cello warm-up tunes.

I break into a run again.

A narrow set of stairs off the gym leads to a basement hallway. I've never been down here. There's no reason at all to be on this level, except maybe if you wanted to play Truth or Dare—or find a dog.

The harp has stopped playing. "Nicholas?" I call. "Dibs?"

I squint through the gloom. I feel so

far from the Pumpkin Patch. In a way, I also feel far from the school, even though technically I'm still inside it. The basement is different from the upper floor. It's like a honeycomb of many tiny rooms. The windows are high-up rectangles, where you get a view of people's feet.

One room stores balls and hula hoops and soccer goals.

Another has all the AV equipment.

Floom, floom, floom! Harp music floats from the end of the hall.

I gulp a breath as I wheel around the corner. "Helloooo?"

In a dark alcove, jam-packed with stored instruments, music stands, and filing cabinets, there's Nicholas, sitting behind a huge harp, strumming away.

And at his feet—is Dibs! I drop to my knees to kiss my precious pet's lopsided star marking, and then I throw my arms around him, burying my face in scruffy soft Dibsness. My relief is pouring out in my hug.

"What happened?" I whisper. "Also, why am I whispering?"

"Given must have had her eye on Dibs for the whole day," Nicholas tells me. "We unclipped her leash for some more pictures, and then she jumped off the table. I followed her all the way into the school, through the back entrance. She led me right to Dibs, who was wandering around the gym." Nicholas is still whispering. "Dibs was so glad to see Given he chased her down the steps, and we all ended up here. I had two pets, no leashes—and then Given jumped up on the filing cabinet and"—Nicholas points—"into that crawl space." He sighs. "So now we've got a cat trapped inside the walls of Boggs Hollow."

"Better than a ghost," I say.

"If you don't rescue her, she might become one," says Nicholas.

"I'm glad I heard you," I say. "The school is practically deserted."

"Well, I didn't know what else to do," says Nicholas. "It's not like I could just leave to get help, because I couldn't take my eyes off Given even for a second. You wouldn't disappear on us, wouldja, Given?" Nicholas asks softly.

"Actually, she would so totally do that. She loves an adventure, just like me." I fold my arms and step back, thinking. "Climbing a filing cabinet is a little bit like climbing a tree, right?"

"Don't ask me," says Nicholas. "I've never climbed a tree in my life."

When I stand on my tiptoes, I see a bit of Given's curled tail in the crawl space. "I bet, like if she was up in a tree, Given wants to come down but doesn't know how." I just have to decide this tall filing cabinet is a tree. "You're a tree," I tell it, to get it ready. Nicholas watches as I stretch myself from the stepladder to the plastic bin to the cabinet. I can do this, right? Firefighters climb for cats all the time!

But now that I'm kneeling on the very top of the cabinet, I feel woozy. I'm glad there is no poster with safety rules here. I am probably breaking a lot of them.

I edge my hand up carefully. Wriggle my fingers. "Given. It's just me."

From inside, I hear a tiny meow.

Another inch of my hand, and I'm rewarded with a brush of whiskers, an inquisitive pink nose, and then—Given leaps out of the crawl space and onto my lap, carrying such a cloud of lint and dust that a sneeze rockets out of me.

She feels like a warm, heavy powder puff in my arms. When she stares up at me and meows, I am pretty sure it's a thank-you.

"Good tree climbing," says Nicholas.

By the next second, Given has jumped down into Nicholas's arms.

"It's going to take me a few more minutes to get down from here," I say. "Last I checked, I don't have any cat-pouncing chromosomes."

Slow and steady, and holding in my sneezes, I get there. Once I'm safe on the ground, cleaning the dust off my glasses, Nicholas says, "Thanks, Becket, for rescuing my cat."

"Thanks to you, Given, for finding my dog," I say, popping my glasses back on to look at our pets. They both make me feel so good inside, like I'm made out of melted cotton candy.

"Good teamwork," says Nicholas. "Given followed Dibs, and I

followed Given, and you followed my music. And now we all can go home together."

We smile at each other and say, at the same time: "Many Branches, one tree!"

CHAPTER 20

Two Two, Ten Ten

LATER, AFTER WE'RE ALL HOME FROM THE PUMPKIN PATCH, Mom, Dad, and I take Dibs out to the back lawn to practice Sit and Stay. Dibs mostly does fine, but I have a feeling that "training Dibs" is a chore that will remain on the board for a while.

"We really need to get Stay down cold. A missing pet is more adventure than this family needs," says Mom, who still doesn't look like she's totally recovered from our story of the carrier-escape dog and the cat in the crawl space.

After dinner, Dad heats up mugs of apple cider and the whole family goes out to the back porch to look at the sky full of stars. Nicholas brings Clive down for an outdoor concert. Starry nights and cello music go together like cider and cinnamon sticks.

"You're getting good, Nicholas," says Dad.

"Puts a tear in my eye," says Gran.

"It's the Branch family's biggest Beautiful Alert of the fall," I say.

Dibs nudges his pink ball over to me. For the millionth time, I toss it, and for the first time ever, he catches it and balances it on the tip of his nose.

"He did it!" I am truly amazed.

"And, Caroline, you didn't even have your phone! I can run in and get it for you?" If I had a photo of Dibs doing something bedazzling, then maybe it could go up in the online Pumpkin Patch photos—or we could use it as a holiday card! "I bet I can get him to do it again."

"No, no. I don't want to take any more pictures today." Caroline sips her cider.

"Besides, *we* saw," says Gran.

"Maybe that's all the audience that Dibs needs," says Nicholas. "Same as me."

"Dibs does remind me of you," I say. "He saves his bedazzling for the family. He likes a peaceful, low-key atmosphere."

"But Given is more like you," says Nicholas. "She shines when there's a lot going on. 'The more, the merrier'—that's Given's motto."

"We each picked a pet to match each other, instead of ourselves," I say.

"Maybe because you knew that's the pet that fits you best," says Mom.

Then Caroline and Gran go inside and come back out holding a plate of lemon loaf, all lit up in birthday candles. It's a do-over!

Everyone sings the happy birthday song, and when Nicholas and I blow out the candles together, it feels like the real start to the Best Branch Year Yet.

Later, upstairs, Dibs and I make our goodnight rounds. Caroline is on the phone, but she smiles and makes a knocking motion to say that she will come to my room later.

Nicholas is in bed, in his lumberjack pajamas, playing with his fidget spinner. Has he figured out what's different about his room yet? Then I notice something else new—a framed photograph centered on his bureau, between our old baby album photo and his globe.

"It's Gran's photo of Maxwell and Maxine," I say. "And, look, now that it's framed, it's bigger than a grapefruit."

"Gran said I could have it," says Nicholas. "It makes the room homier, right? Especially since I'm sleeping here all by myself."

"You're not sleeping all by yourself," I say. "Check under your bed."

Nicholas looks scared. "It's not another mouse, is it?"

"No! It's way better than a mouse."

He gets out of bed to look. I look, too, even though I know what I will see—Given's eyes peeking out of her plaid sleeping saucer.

"You moved Given's bed to under my bed!" says Nicholas. His smile has taken over his face. "What made you think of doing that?"

"Well, Given brought the mouse here, right? And she's always sitting on your windowsill, or she's hiding under your bed. She knows you're her person, Nicholas. She's pretty much your roommate already."

"No matter how much attention Given is given all day, while I'm sleeping, she's with me," says Nicholas quietly. "When she's not on the prowl, her sleep saucer is always her home base."

"Nicholas, do you realize that next year, we turn eleven on the tenth day of the tenth month?"

"Yes," he says. "So?"

"Eleven plus eleven is twenty-two," I say. "Two two."

"So?"

"Two two, ten ten," I say triumphantly. "How cool is that? That only happens once in a lifetime! It's the most incredible, special birth date I could ever imagine! And I was thinking if we start planning it now, we can make our Two Two, Ten Ten party exactly the way we want. Something with the exactly right amount of same and opposite, and the just-right balance of you and me."

"Count me in," he says. When I fling out my arms to hug him, I knock his fidget spinner out of his hand. Nicholas catches it just in time, and hugs me back.

Acknowledgments

Writing about the world of Becket Branch is a dream come true. After all, it's a chance to follow my favorite fictional family through another season, and this time with new characters and pets for extra bounce and pounce. Thank you, Elise Howard, Sarah Alpert, and Elizabeth Johnson, for all your Beautiful Alert thoughts and care of Becket's story. Thank you, LeUyen Pham, for bringing Becket to life. Thank you, Emily van Beek, Sarah Mlynowski, and Courtney Sheinmel, for those early reads. And a big hug to my real-life family—Erich, Jason, Hace, Toby, and Trudy—for inspiring me to write about love, laughter, and lasagna. What fun!